RANDOM HOUSE
CHILDREN'S BOOKS

Dear Educator:

A magical cupboard. A new friend from another time and place. An important secret to keep. These are just a few elements of the Indian in the Cupboard books—*The Indian in the Cupboard, The Return of the Indian,* and *The Secret of the Indian*—that will entice young readers to join Omri on his adventures.

When Omri puts a plastic Indian brave into a metal cupboard and locks the door with a mysterious skeleton key, the Indian is transformed into a real live man and Omri's life changes forever. Not only are these books classic fantasy adventure, but they also touch on themes perfect for classroom discussion, including friendship, trust, secrets, responsibility, growing up, stereotypes, and bullying.

You have in your hands an exclusive Teachers Edition with the complete text of *The Return of the Indian,* an extensive educator guide for all three books, and an interview with author Lynne Reid Banks. I hope that you spark your students' imaginations with these enchanting books.

Best wishes,

Lisa Nadel

Lisa Nadel
Senior Manager, Educational Marketing

The
RETURN
of the
INDIAN

The
RETURN
of the
INDIAN

Lynne Reid Banks

Illustrated by William Geldart

A YEARLING BOOK

Text copyright © 1986 by Lynne Reid Banks
Illustrations copyright © 1986 by William Geldart

All rights reserved. Published in the United States by Yearling, an imprint of Random House Children's Books, a division of Random House, Inc., New York. Originally published in hardcover by Doubleday, an imprint of Random House Children's Books, in 1986.

Yearling and the jumping horse design are registered trademarks of Random House, Inc.

Visit us on the Web! www.randomhouse.com/kids

Educators and librarians, for a variety of teaching tools, visit us at www.randomhouse.com/teachers

The Library of Congress has cataloged the hardcover edition of this work as follows:
Banks, Lynne Reid.
The Return of the Indian / Banks, Lynne Reid.
p. cm.
Summary: A year after he sends his Indian friend, Little Bear, back into the magic cupboard, Omri decides to bring him back only to find that he is close to death and in need of help.
Sequel to "The Indian in the Cupboard."
ISBN: 978-0-385-23497-9 (trade)
[1. Indians of North America—Fiction. 2. Toys—Fiction. 3. Magic—Fiction.]
I. Geldart, Bill. II. Title.
PZ7.B2262Re 1986
[Fic]—dc19
85031119

ISBN: 978-0-375-86033-1

Printed in the United States of America

10 9 8 7 6 5 4 3 2 1
First Yearling Edition

To all those who wrote to me,
giving me ideas!

Contents

Contents

The
RETURN
of the
INDIAN

1

A Defeat

O MRI EMERGED CAUTIOUSLY from the station into Hove Road.

Someone with a sense of humor and a black spray can had recently added an *L* to the word "Hove" on the street sign on the corner, making it "Hovel Road." Omri thought grimly that this was much more appropriate than "Hove," which sounded pleasantly like somewhere by the sea. Omri would have liked to live by the sea, or indeed almost anywhere in the world rather than Hovel Road. He had done his best to understand why his parents had decided to move here from the other house in the other, much nicer, neighborhood. True, the new house was larger, and so was the garden. But the area was a slum.

Omri's father objected strongly to Omri's calling it a slum. But then, *he* had a car. He didn't have to walk half a mile along Hovel Road to the station every day, as Omri did to get to school, and again—as now—to get home in the gloomy afternoon. It was October and the clocks had gone back. That meant that when he came out of the station it was practically dark.

Omri was only one of many children walking, playing or hanging around in Hovel Road at this hour, but he was the only one who wore school uniform. Of course he took his blazer and tie off in the train and stuffed them into his schoolbag, but that still left his white shirt, black trousers and gray pullover. However he mussed them up, he still stood out among the others he had to pass through.

These others all went to a local school where uniform was not required. Under other circumstances, Omri would have begged his parents to let him change schools. At least then he wouldn't have been an obvious outsider. Or maybe he would. He couldn't imagine going to school with these kids. After a term and a half of running the gauntlet of their mindless antagonism every working day, he regarded them as little better than a pack of wolves.

That group waiting for him on the corner by the amusement arcade. He knew them by now, and they knew him. They waited for him if they had nothing better to do. His passing seemed to be one of the highlights of their day.

Their faces positively lit up as they saw him approach. It took all his courage to keep walking towards them.

At moments like this, he would remember Little Bear. Little Bear had been only a fraction of Omri's size, and yet he had stood up to him. If he had felt scared, as Omri did now, he never showed it. Omri was not that much smaller than these boys. There were just so many of them, and only one of him. But imagine if they'd been giants, as he was to Little Bear! They were nothing but kids like himself, although several years older. Except that they weren't like him. "They're rats," he thought, to rouse himself for battle. "Pigs. Toads. Mad dogs." It would be shameful to let them see he was afraid of them. He gripped his schoolbag tightly by both handles and came on.

If only he had had Boone's revolver, or Little Bear's knife, or his bow and arrows, or his ax. If only he could fight like a cowboy or an Indian brave! How he would show that crew then!

The boy he had to pass first was a skinhead, like several of the others. The cropped head made him look somehow animal-like. He had a flat, whitish face and about five gold rings in one ear. Omri should have detoured a bit to be out of range, but he would not swerve from his path. The skinhead's boot shot out, but Omri was expecting that and skipped over it. Then a concerted movement by the others jerked Omri into evasive action. Speed was his only hope. He broke into a run, hampered by his heavy bag.

Several hands reached out to grab him as he passed. One caught and held fast. He swung the bag and it hit home. The boy released his hold, doubled over and said, "Uuoogh!" It reminded Omri of the time Little Bear had fought Boone, the cowboy, and got kicked in the stomach—he'd made the same noise.

Someone else clutched Omri's flying shirttail and he jerked away hard and heard it rip. He swung around with his bag again, missed, found himself turning in a circle after the bag. There was the sound of jeering laughter. He felt hot rage flood under his skin. He was roused now, he wanted to stop, to fight; but he saw their sneering, idiot faces. That was all they were waiting for. They would beat him up—they'd done it once before and he had stumbled

home with a bloody nose and a shoulder bruised from the pavement, and one shoe missing. His schoolbag, too. He'd had to go back (Adiel, the elder of his two brothers, had gone with him) and found all his books scattered and the bag torn and half full of garbage.

An experience like that taught you something. He fled, hating himself but hating his enemies worse. They didn't pursue him. That would have been too much trouble. But their shouts and jeers followed him all the way to his gate.

As he turned into it, he slowed down. He was on safe ground here. It was a different world. The property had a high hedge which shut it off from the street. The house was a nice house, Omri didn't deny that. He could see into the warm, well-lit living room, with its familiar furniture and lamps and ornaments and pictures.

His mother was in there, just putting a match to the open fire. Omri paused in the twilight to watch. He loved to see the flames. These, too, reminded him of Little Bear and the tiny fires he had made outside his tepee, the love dance he had done around his fire when he had married Bright Stars . . . Omri sighed. It was over a year since that time. But not a single day had passed without his thinking about his Indian and all the astonishing adventures they had had together.

Omri had grown up quite a bit in the meantime. There had been moments when he would almost have liked to believe that he'd made the whole thing up. A plastic Indian coming alive—absurd! He had tried to push it to the back of his mind, but it wouldn't be pushed. It was as vividly real to him as if it had happened this morning.

The little bathroom cupboard. His special key, which his mother had given him. And magic. The magic that brought plastic people to life . . . It *had* happened, all of it . . . And yet, three days ago, Patrick had behaved in that peculiar way. It had shaken Omri, shaken his belief in his own memory.

Patrick, too, had moved out of the old neighborhood. When his parents got divorced, he and his mother and brother had gone right away. This had happened months ago. At first the boys had written to each other, but somehow the letters had petered out. There'd been no contact between them. Until, three days ago, Omri had been walking out the school gate (their old school—Omri was now in his final year before high school) and found Patrick waiting for him.

Patrick had grown. He looked different in the face as well. They just stood in front of each other, grinning, not knowing what to say.

"How've you been?" said Patrick at last.

"All right," said Omri. "Have you moved back?"

"No. We're visiting. I thought I'd come and look at the old school."

They had begun walking towards the station.

"Do you like where you live now?" Omri had asked.

"Oh yeah, the country's all right. Once you get used to it. I've made a few friends. And the cottage is nice. Seems funny with just the three of us." Omri didn't press this point. He could hardly imagine life without *his* dad, but then, his dad didn't hit him, or hit his mother.

They chatted on rather awkwardly, with some silences, but it got better. By the time they'd reached the station it was almost as if Patrick had never gone away, as if they were still as close as they used to be. That was why Omri didn't hesitate to say, "Where do you keep Boone and his horse?"

Patrick seemed to stumble as he walked, like a hiccup with his feet.

"Who?"

A little cold shiver passed down Omri's back. He stopped. "Boone."

Patrick stopped too. He stared across Omri's shoulder at the station. "What are you on about? Who's Boone?"

Omri narrowed his eyes. Could Patrick be serious, or was he teasing? But Patrick wasn't a tease. "You know perfectly well. Your cowboy." There was a silence. Patrick was rubbing his thumb against the side of his finger, a quick, dry, nervous sound. "Like Little Bear was my Indian," said Omri. He couldn't quite believe what seemed to be happening, so

7

he rattled on, "I've still got *him*, of course. The plastic figure of him, I mean. Remember? How he sat on his pony with Bright Stars in front of him, and raised his hand to say good-bye just as we shut the cupboard door, when we sent them back?"

The silence went on for what seemed like eternity. Then Patrick snapped his head around and looked into Omri's face. "You're talking a load of rubbish," he said loudly. "I gave you a plastic Indian for your birthday. That's all I remember." He looked at his watch. "My mum's waiting," he said shortly. "Bye." And he ran off.

Now as Omri stood outside his new house in the gathering dark, a possible solution to this troubling and incredible episode came to him.

Maybe Patrick doesn't want to remember, he thought. Because a thing like that, well . . . it makes you different from other people. It's a secret you can never tell, not if you don't want everyone to think you're crazy. It's lonely having a secret like that. If Patrick hadn't moved away, if they could have kept talking about it and remembering *together*, then he'd never have denied it, or started trying to pretend it never happened.

2

A Victory

OMRI ENTERED THE HOUSE by the side door, which opened into the kitchen. His black and white cat, Kitsa, was sitting on the drainboard. She watched him out of her knowing green eyes as he came to get a drink of water.

"You're not supposed to be up there, Kits," he said, "you know that." She continued to stare at him. He flicked some water on her but she ignored it. He laughed and stroked her head. He was crazy about her. He loved her independence and disobedience.

He helped himself to a hunk of bread, butter and Primula cheese, and walked through into the breakfast room. It was their every-meal room, actually. Omri sat down and opened the paper to the cartoon. Kitsa came in, and jumped, not onto his knee but onto the table, where she lay down on the newspaper right over the bit he was looking at. She was always doing this—she couldn't bear to see people reading.

Omri felt tired. It had been a long day. He laid his head on his arm, bringing it level with Kitsa's face, and communed with her, eyeball to eyeball. He felt sleepy and cat-like. When his mother came bursting in, it gave him a fright.

"Oh, Mum . . . I wish you wouldn't bash about like that!"

"Omri!"

He looked at her. She had a strange look on her face. Her eyes and mouth were wide open and she was staring at him as if she'd never seen him before.

He sat up straight, his heart beating. "What's up?"

"A letter came for you," she said in an odd voice to match her goggle-eyed expression.

"A letter? For me? Who from?"

"I—I'm afraid I opened it."

She came over to him and gave him a long envelope, torn open at the top. It had printing on it as well as his name and address in typing. Omri started at it. It said, "Telecom—*Your* Communications Service." He felt numb inside. It couldn't be. *It couldn't be.* He didn't touch the letter, which lay on the table beside Kitsa. For once, his mother didn't even seem to notice that she was there—normally she chased her off.

"Why did you open it?" Omri asked at last in a croaky voice.

"Darling, because I didn't look at the name. You boys don't get many letters." She gave a short, rather hysterical laugh. Omri quite saw how it could happen. He just wished . . . he wished he could have been the first to know.

"Well, go on—read it!"

He picked up the envelope and took out the letter.

> *Dear Omri,*
>
> *We are delighted to inform you that your story, "The Plastic Indian," has won first prize for your age group in our Telecom Creative Writing Competition.*
>
> *We think it is a superb story, showing extraordinary powers of imagination and invention. Our judges consider it worthy of publication.*
>
> *Your prize, £300.00, will be presented to you at a party we are giving for all prize winners on November 25th in the Savoy Hotel. A special invitation card will be sent to you.*
>
> *May we congratulate you on your success.*
>
> *Yours sincerely,*
>
> *Squiggle Squiggle,*
>
> COMPETITION DIRECTOR FOR TELECOM

Omri kept his eyes on this letter long after he had finished reading it. Inside, he was jumping up from his chair, running around and around the room, hugging his mother, shouting with triumph. But in reality he just sat there staring at the letter, a deep glow like hot coals in his chest, too happy and astonished to move or speak. He didn't even notice that his free hand was stroking Kitsa from nose tip to tail tip again and again while she lay on the newspaper, purring with bliss.

His mother woke him from his trance.

"Darling? Do you realize? Isn't it fantastic? And you never said a single word!"

At this moment his father came in from outdoors. He'd been working in the garden, as he often did, until it was actually too dark to see. Now he stamped the mud off his shoes in the open doorway, but, for once, Omri's mother didn't care about the mud, and fairly dragged him into the room.

"Oh, do come and hear the news! I've been bursting to tell you all day—Omri—tell him, tell him—"

Wordlessly, Omri handed his father the letter. There was a silence, then his father breathed reverently, "God in Heaven. Three hundred pounds!"

"It's not the *money*!" cried his mother. "Look, look what they say about his *story*! He must be *brilliant*, and we never even knew he had writing talent!" She came to Omri and smothered him with hugs. "When can we read it? Oh, just wait till the boys hear about this—"

His brothers! Yes. That would be almost the sweetest thing of all. They always behaved as if he were too thick to do anything. And telling them at school. His English teacher simply wouldn't believe her senses. Perhaps Mr. Johnson, the headmaster, would get him up at Assembly and announce the news, and they would all applaud, and he would be asked to read the story aloud . . . Omri's head began to spin with the incredible excitement of it. He jumped up.

"I'll go and get my copy and you can read it," he said.

"Oh, did you keep a copy?"

"Yes, that was in the rules." He stopped in the doorway and turned. "I typed it on your typewriter when you were out," he confessed.

"Did you, indeed! That must have been the time I found all the keys jumbled together." But she wasn't a bit annoyed.

"And I borrowed paper and carbon paper from Dad's desk. And a big envelope to send it in."

His mother and father looked at each other. They were both absolutely beaming with pride, as they had when Gillon had come home and announced he'd broken a swimming record at school, and when Adiel had passed ten O-level exams. Omri, looking at them, knew suddenly that he had never expected them to have that look because of him.

"Well," said his father, very solemnly, "now you can pay me back. That will be eleven and a half pence you owe me." His face broke into a great soppy grin.

Omri raced upstairs. His heart was pounding. He'd won. He'd actually won! He'd never dared to hope he would. Of course, he'd dreamed a bit. After all, he had tried his very best, and it *was* a great story to begin with. "Imagination and invention," eh? That was all they knew. The real work was in the way he'd written it, and rewritten it, and checked the spelling until just for once he could be confident that every word was right. He'd gotten Adiel to help with that part—without telling him, of course, what it was actually for.

"Stirrup? Maize? Iroquois?"

"*Iroquois!*" Adiel had exclaimed.

"It's the name of an Indian tribe," said Omri. Fancy not knowing that! Omri had now read so many books about American Indians that he'd forgotten that not everyone was as knowledgeable on the subject as himself.

"Well, I haven't a clue how to spell it. I-R-O-K-W-"

"No, it's not—it's like French. Never mind, I know that one, I just wanted to see if you did. Whiskey?"

Adiel spelt it, and then asked, "What on earth is this you're writing? What a weird bunch of words!"

"It's a story. I've got to get it as good as I can."

"But what's it about? Let me see it," said Adiel, making a grab at the notebook.

Omri dodged. "Leave off! I'll show you when it's finished. Now. Bandage?" Adiel spelt this (actually Omri had it right) and then Omri hesitated before saying, "cupboard?"

Adiel's eyes narrowed.

"You're not telling about the time I hid your so-called secret cupboard after you'd nicked my football shorts—"

"I didn't—"

"The time the key got lost and you made such an idiotic uproar? You're not going to put *me* into any stupid school story."

"I'm changing the names," said Omri.

"You'd better. Any more words?"

Omri read on silently to the next longish word. "Magnanimous."

"Wow," said Adiel with heavy sarcasm. "Bet you don't even know what it means."

"Yes I do: generous."

"Where'd you get it from?"

"'The Iroquois were a tribe ferocious in war, stalwart in alliance, magnanimous in victory,'" quoted Omri.

"You sound like Winston Churchill," said Adiel, but there was a trace of admiration in his voice this time.

"Don't make it too show-offy, will you? You'll only lose marks if your teacher thinks you've copied it."

"I haven't *written* that, you *jerk*," said Omri, "I'm just remembering what I've read in a book." He was beginning to relish long words, though. Later, he went through his story yet again to make sure he hadn't used too many. His teacher was forever saying, "Keep it simple. Stick to what you know." Little would anyone guess how closely he had stuck to the truth this time!

And now . . . "Imagination and invention" . . .

He paused on the stairs. Had he cheated? It was supposed to be a made-up story. It said so in the rules. Or had it? "Creative writing" meant that, didn't it? You couldn't create something that had really happened . . . All you could do was find the best way of writing it down. Of course he had had to make up bits of it; vivid as his memories of Little Bear and Boone were, he couldn't remember every word they ever spoke. Omri frowned. He didn't feel entirely easy in his mind, but on the other hand . . . Nobody had helped him. The way he'd written the story was all his own. Maybe it was okay. There wasn't much he could do about it anyhow.

He continued more slowly up the stairs to his own room, at the very top of the house.

3

The Way It Began

OMRI WAS RATHER a private person. At least, he needed to be alone quite a bit of the time. So his room, which was right up under the eaves of the house, was perfect for him.

In the old house, his bedroom had been just one of several opening off the upstairs landing, and at certain times of the day had been like a railway station. His new room was off the beaten track. No one (in his opinion) had any reason to come up here, or even pass the door. There were times, now that he had it all arranged to suit himself, when he forgot about how awful it was living in Hovel Road, when it seemed worth anything to have a room like this.

It wasn't a very large room, so his father had built a

shelf high up under the skylight for him to sleep on. This was great, because he could look up at the night sky. Under this bed shelf were his desk and more shelves for his collections of old bottles, key rings and wooden animals. The wall opposite the window was covered with his posters—a mixture of old and new, from Snoopy and an early Beatles, to the Police and a funny one about a flasher who gets caught in an elevator. In pride of place were two large photographs of Iroquois chieftains that he'd found in magazines. Neither of these Indians looked remotely like Little Bear, but they appealed to Omri just the same.

His clothes were stored on the landing, so his room wasn't cluttered up with them. That left quite a lot of space for his beanbag seats, a low table (he'd sawed its legs to half their length after seeing a photo of a Japanese room), his cassette radio, and his most recent acquisition: an old chest.

He'd found this in the local market, coated with dirt and grease, bought it for £2 after bargaining, and borrowed a cart from a marketman to drag it around the corner to Hovel Road. He'd cleaned it with a scraper and some sandpaper out in the garden, before hauling it up to his room.

It had "come up a treat," just as the man in the market had promised. The wood was oak, the hinges iron, and it had a brass plate on it with the name of its first owner. Omri had hardly been able to believe it when he had removed the layers of dirt from this plate and read the name for the first time. It was L. Bear. L. Bear . . . Little Bear! Of course it was pure coincidence, but, as Omri thought, "If I were superstitious—!" He shined the brass every week. Somehow it, too, made him feel closer to Little Bear.

The chest was not only interesting and beautiful, but useful. Omri used it for storage. There was only one thing wrong with it. It had a lock, but no key. So he piled cushions and other objects on it and pretended it was a bench. That way, nobody who happened to be prying about in his room (it still happened occasionally, mothers cleaning and brothers poking about "borrowing") would realize that it contained a number of interesting and private objects.

Omri knelt by the chest now and shifted to the floor a pile of cassettes, a Bullworker (he was bent on developing his muscles), some cushions and three copies of *Mad* magazine, among other bits of junk. Then he opened the lid of the chest. It, too, was untidy, but Omri knew where to burrow. On their way down the left-hand side in search of the folder containing his prize-winning story, Omri's fingers touched metal, and paused. Then, carefully, he moved some other things which were in the way, and eased this metal object out.

It was a small white cabinet with a mirror in its door and a keyhole—an old-fashioned bathroom medicine cupboard in fact. He stood it on the Japanese table. The door swung open. Apart from a single shelf, it was quite empty—as empty as it had been when he'd first received it, a rather odd birthday present from Gillon, just over a year ago.

Omri sat back on his heels staring at it.

How clearly it all came back! The cupboard. The strange little key, which had been his great-grandmother's, and which had mysteriously fitted the commonplace lock and turned this ordinary little metal box into a time machine with a difference. Put any plastic object—an ax, an Indian tepee, a quiver of arrows—into it, close the door, turn the key . . . and those things became real—miniature but real. Real leather, real cloth, real steel. Put the plastic figures of human beings or animals inside, and in the time it took to lock them in, they, too, became real. Real and alive. And not just "living toys," but people from another time, from their own lives, with their own personalities and needs and demands . . .

Oh, it hadn't been all fun and games, as Omri had naively expected at first. Little Bear was no toy, to submit tamely to being played with. He was, for all his tiny stature, a ferocious savage, warlike and domineering.

Omri had soon realized that if any grown-ups found out about the cabinet's magic properties, they would take it, and the Indian and everything else, away. So Omri had had to keep it secret, and look after, feed and protect his

Indian as best he could. And when Patrick had found out the secret and sneaked a Texas cowboy into the cupboard so that he, too, could have a "little person," the trouble really started.

Little Bear and Boone were natural enemies. They came close to killing each other several times. Even their respective ponies had caused endless difficulties. And then Adiel had taken the cupboard one day, the key had fallen out of the lock and been lost, and Omri, Patrick and the two little men had been faced with the dire possibility that the magic was dead, that these minute and helpless people would have to remain in Omri's time, his "giant" world, and in his care, forever . . .

It was this, the terrible fright they had all had from this notion, that had finally proved to Omri that he would have to give up his Indian friend (for friends they were by then, of a sort) and send the little people "back"—back to their own time, through the magic of the cupboard. When the key was found, that's what they all agreed on. But it was so hard to part that Boone (who was shamingly softhearted for a cowboy) had cried openly, and even the boys' eyes were wet . . . Omri seldom let himself think of those last moments, they upset him so much.

When they'd reopened the cupboard door, there were the two groups: Little Bear and the wife Omri had found him, Bright Stars, sitting on Little Bear's pony, and "Boo-

Hoo" Boone on his white horse—only now they were plastic again. Patrick had taken Boone and put him in his pocket. And Omri had kept the Indians. He had them still. He had packed them in a little wooden box which he kept safely at the very bottom of the chest. Actually it was a box within a box within a box. Each was tied tightly with string. There was a reason for all this. Omri had wanted to make them difficult to get at.

He had always known that he would be tempted to put Little Bear and Bright Stars into the cupboard again and bring them back to life. His curiosity about how they were getting on—that alone tormented him every day. They had lived in dangerous times, times of war between tribes, wars aided and encouraged by Frenchmen and Englishmen who were fighting on American soil in those far-off days. Boone's time, the time of the pioneering of Texas, a hundred years after Little Bear's era, was dangerous too.

And there'd been another little man, Tommy the British medical orderly from the First World War—they'd magicked him to life to help when Little Bear was kicked by his horse, when Boone was dying of an arrow wound . . . Tommy might, just might still be alive in Omri's world, but he would be terribly old, about ninety by now.

By putting their plastic figures into the magic cupboard, by turning the magic key, Omri had the power to recall them to life. To youth. He could snatch them from the past. The whole business nearly blew Omri's mind every time he thought at all deeply about it. So he tried not to think about it too much. And to prevent his yielding to temptation, he had given his mother the key. She wore it around her neck on a chain (it was quite decorative). People often asked her about it, and she would say, "It's Omri's really, but he lends it to me." That wasn't the whole truth. Omri had pressed it on her and begged her to keep it safe for him. Safe . . . not just from getting lost again, but safe *from him*, from his longing to use it again; to reactivate the magic, to bring back his friends. To bring back the time when he had been—not happiest, but most intensely, dangerously alive himself.

4

The Sweet Taste of Triumph

WHEN OMRI CAME BACK downstairs with the copy of his story, his brothers were both back from school.

Noticing that their parents were fairly gibbering with excitement, they were both pestering loudly to be told what had happened, but, being decent, Omri's mother and father were refusing to spoil his surprise. However, the moment he entered the room his father turned and pointed to him.

"It's Omri's news," he said. "Ask him to tell you."

"Well?" said Gillon.

"Go on," said Adiel. "Don't drive us mad."

"It's just that I've won a prize," said Omri with the utmost carelessness. "Here, Mum." He handed her the folder, and she rushed out of the room with it clutched to her bosom, saying that she couldn't wait another minute to read it.

"Prize for what?" asked Adiel cynically.

"For winning a donkey race?" inquired Gillon.

"Nothing much, it was only a story," said Omri. It was such a long time since he had felt this good, he needed to spin it out.

"What story?" asked Adiel.

"What's the prize?" asked Gillon at the same time.

"You know, that Telecom competition. There was an ad on TV. You had to write in for a leaflet from the post office."

"Oh, that," said Adiel, and went into the kitchen to get himself something to eat.

But Gillon was gazing at him. He paid more attention to ads, and he had remembered a detail that Adiel had forgotten.

"The prizes were money," he said slowly. "Big money."

Omri grunted noncommittally, sat down at the table and shifted Kitsa, who was still there, onto his lap.

"How much?" pressed Gillon.

"Hm?"

"How much?—Did you *win*? You didn't get first prize?"

"Yeah."

Gillon got up. "Not—you haven't won three hundred quid?"

Adiel's face appeared around the kitchen door, wearing a look of comical amazement.

"WHAT! What did you say?"

"That was the first prize in each category. I thought about entering myself." Excitement and envy were in Gillon's voice now, making it wobble up and down the register. He turned back to Omri. "Come on! Tell us."

"Yeah," said Omri again.

He felt their eyes on him and a great gleeful laugh rising in him, like the time Boone had done a tiny brilliant drawing during Omri's art lesson and the teacher had seen it and couldn't believe her eyes. She'd thought Omri had done it somehow. This time was even more fun, though, because this time he *had*.

He was sitting watching television some time later, when Adiel came in quietly and sat down beside him.

"I've read it," he said after a while. His tone had changed completely.

"What?—Oh, my Indian story."

"Yes. Your Indian story." There was a pause, and then Adiel—his exam-passing brother—said very sincerely, almost humbly, "It's one of the best stories I've ever read."

Omri turned to look at him. "Do you really like it?" he asked eagerly. Whatever rows he might have with his brothers, and he had them daily, their good opinion mattered. Adiel's especially.

"You know perfectly well it's brilliant. How on earth

did you dream all that up? Coming from another time and all that? It's so well worked out, so . . . I dunno. You actually had me *believing* in it. And working in all those real parts, about the family. Blimey. I mean it was terrific. I . . . now don't take this the wrong way, but I can't quite credit that you made it all up."

After a pause, Omri said, "What do you mean? That you think I nicked it from a book? Because I didn't."

"It's entirely original?"

Omri glanced at him. "Original? Yes. That's what it is. It's original."

"Well, congratulations, anyway. I think it's fabulous." They stared at the screen for a while and then he added, "You'd better go and talk to Mum. She's sobbing her eyes out."

Omri reluctantly went in search of his mother, and found her in the conservatory at the back of the house watering her plants. Not with tears—to his great relief she was not crying now, but she gave him a rather misty smile and said, "I read the story, Omri. It's utterly amazing. No wonder it won. You're the darkest little horse I ever knew and I love you." She hugged him. He submitted briefly, then politely extricated himself.

"When's supper?"

"Usual time."

He was just turning to go when he stopped and looked

at her again. Something was missing from her general appearance. Then he saw what it was, and his heart missed a beat.

"Mum! Where's the key?"

Her hand went to her neck.

"Oh . . . I took it off this morning when I washed my hair. It's in the upstairs bathroom."

Omri didn't mean to run, but he couldn't help it. He had to see the key, to be sure it wasn't lost. He pelted up the stairs and into his parents' bathroom. The key was there! He saw it as soon as he went in, lying on the ledge beside the basin with its silver chain coiled around it.

He picked it up. It was the first time he'd held it for a year. It felt colder and lighter than he remembered. Its twisted top and complicated lock part clicked into place in some memory pattern. And something else clicked at the same time, something that had been hovering in his mind, undefined, since he'd read the letter.

His story *was* original. Adiel had relieved his mind when he'd used that word. Even if you didn't make a story up, if *you* had the experience, and *you* wrote about it, it was original. So he hadn't cheated. But the story wasn't only his. It also belonged to the little men—to Little Bear, and Boone, and even to Tommy, the World War I soldier. (It belonged to Patrick, too, but if Patrick had decided to deny it ever happened, then he'd given up his rights in it.)

And suddenly Omri realized, as he looked at the key,

that his triumph wouldn't really be complete until he'd shared it. Not just with his parents and brothers, or with the kids at school. No prize, no party could be as good as what he was thinking about now. This was his reason—his excuse to do what he'd been yearning to do ever since that moment when the cupboard door closed and transformed his friends back into plastic.

Only with Little Bear and Boone could he share the secret behind his story, the most exciting part of all—that it was true.

He turned, went out of the bathroom and up the remaining stairs to his attic room.

Not for long, he was thinking. "I won't bring them back for long. Not long enough to cause problems. Just long enough to have a good talk. To find out how they are."

Maybe Bright Stars had had a baby by now—a papoose! What fun if she brought it with her—though it would be almost too tiny to see. Little Bear had made himself a chief while he was with Omri, but when he returned to his own place, his father might still be alive. Little Bear wouldn't like being an ordinary brave again! And Boone—the "crying cowboy" with a talent for art, a deep dislike of washing, and a heavy thirst . . . It made Omri grin to think of him. Writing about the little men and their adventures had made them so clear in his mind that it hardly seemed necessary to do what he was going to do.

5

From Dangerous Times

WITH HANDS THAT SHOOK, Omri probed into the depths of the chest till he found the box-within-a-box-within-a-box. He eased it out and closed the lid of the chest and put the boxes on top. Reverently he untied the string on the largest box, opened it, took out the next, and repeated the operation.

In the last box, carefully wrapped in cotton, was the plastic group consisting of a brown pony, an Indian brave, and a young Indian woman in a red dress. The brave's left hand was upraised in farewell, his other arm circled the woman's waist and held the rope rein. The woman, her long brown legs hanging on each side of the pony's withers, had her hands buried in its mane. The pony's head was alertly raised, its ears almost meeting above its forelock, its feet braced. Omri felt himself quivering all over as he stood the tiny figures on his hand and stared at them.

"You're coming back," he whispered—as if plastic could hear. But they wouldn't be plastic long!

The cupboard was ready. Omri stood the figures not on its shelf but on its metal floor. Then he took a deep, deep breath as if he were going to dive into a cold, uncertain sea. He fitted the key into the lock, closed the door, and turned it.

Let it still work. Let it—

He barely had time to think his thought before he heard the tiny, familiar sound—minute unshod hoofs drumming and pawing on the metal!

Omri let his breath out in a rush. His heart was thumping and his hand shook.

His fingers were still around the key. In a second he had turned it back and opened the mirrored door. And there they were—

No. No—!

Omri's fists clenched. There was something terribly wrong. The three figures were there, all right. The details of life, which the dull-surfaced plastic blurred, were there again. The shine on the pony's coat, the brilliance of the red dress, the warm sheen of brown, living skin. But—

The pony was right enough. He was prancing and stamping his feet, fretting his head against the rope. As

Omri opened the door and the light fell on him, he pricked his ears again and whickered nervously. On his back sat Bright Stars. But she was no longer in front. She sat back, almost on the pony's haunches. And before her, but lying face down across the pony's back, was a limp, motionless form.

It was Little Bear. Omri knew it, although he couldn't see his face. His head and arms hung down on one side of the horse and his legs on the other. His buckskin leggings were caked with earth and blood. Omri, against his will forcing himself to peer closer, saw to his utter horror where the blood had come from. There were two bullet holes, almost too small to see, high up on his back.

Omri's mouth was wide open with shock. He looked at Bright Stars. She was holding the pony's rein rope now. Her other hand rested on Little Bear's broad shoulders as if to steady him and keep him from sliding off the pony's back. Her face was frenzied. She had no tears in her eyes, but they were so round Omri could see the sparks of light in the whites. Her tiny teeth were clenched in a desperate grimace.

When she saw Omri, she started like a fawn with fear, but then the fear faded from her face. Her hand left Little Bear's back for a moment and reached itself out toward Omri. It was a gesture of frantic appeal. It said, "Help us!" clearer than words. But Omri couldn't move or speak. He had no notion how to help. He only knew that if he didn't, if someone didn't, Little Bear would die. Perhaps . . . perhaps he was dead already! What could he do?

Tommy.

Tommy's medical knowledge was not exactly up to date. How could it be, when he had only been a medical orderly in the First World War? But he was the best idea Omri could come up with, shocked and numbed as he was.

He beckoned Bright Stars forward with one hand, and while she was guiding the pony over the bottom edge of the cupboard, Omri reached back into the smallest box. The plastic figure of the uniformed soldier was at the bottom, complete with his bag with the red cross on it.

As soon as the cupboard was empty, the horse and riders clear of the door, Omri slipped Tommy in and closed it again, turning the key forward and back in a second. That was all the magic took.

"It'll be all right," he said to Bright Stars, as she sat on the pony on the top of the chest near his face. "Tommy will fix him." Then he opened the door again eagerly, and reached his hand in.

The bag was there. And the uniform, neatly folded, with the orderly's cap upside down on top of the pile. And the boots. And the puttees, the khaki bandages they wore around their legs in that war. Neatly rolled, inside the cap. Nothing else.

Omri let out a cry. He slammed the cupboard door to shut out the sight of that neat little pile of clothes, empty of their owner, who no longer needed them. He knew instantly. He knew that Tommy didn't live to be an old man. That one of those big German shells he had talked about, those "Minnies," or perhaps some other weapon, had struck him down. His snubby, cheerful face, his bravery and his gentle hands were gone, with so many thousands of others, into the mud of the trenches.

Omri had never experienced death at close hand. No one he knew well had ever died. An uncle had "jumped the twig," as his father called it, last year, but in Australia. A boy at school had been killed in a car crash, but he wasn't in Omri's class.

The realization of Tommy's death—even a whole year after he had last seen him—came as a ghastly shock. He had no one to share this with—and in any case, there was no time. Standing at his elbow was the pony, tossing his head as if in impatience and heedlessness of anything which delayed attention to his master. Bright Stars' enormous eyes were fixed on him. Waiting. *Trusting*.

Later. He would think about Tommy, and mourn for him, later. Who would understand better than Tommy that you have to look after the wounded before mourning the dead? Rubbing his hand across his mouth, Omri looked around helplessly, and then he faced Bright Stars.

How much English did she know? During her brief time with him, before, he had never spoken directly to her—she had only spoken to Little Bear, in their own language. Now he must make her understand.

"No good," he said slowly. "No help."

She looked blank, although the shining hope faded a little from her face. To make matters plain, Omri opened the cupboard again and took Tommy's plastic figure—which had come back, replacing the pitiful little pile of his uniform—and stood it before the Indian girl. She slipped from the pony's back and, holding the rope, touched the figure.

She seemed to realize at once that there was no help to be looked for there. She turned swiftly back toward Omri.

"Help. You," she said in a clear, silvery voice.

Omri felt sheer desperation clamp down on his heart, already heavy with sadness. He followed Bright Stars' pointing finger at the lifeless-looking body across the pony.

"We must lay him flat," he said at last. It was all he could think of. But it could not be all he could do. He must think—he must think!

He watched Bright Stars struggling to lift Little Bear's heavy body off the horse. He helped as much as he dared, terrified his big clumsy fingers would damage him, but at least he could make his hand into a kind of platform to lower Little Bear to the ground. With his other hand he pulled his box of tissues toward him and made a makeshift mattress out of several of them. At least they were soft and clean. Soon Little Bear was lying stretched on his stomach.

Omri had been through something like this before. When Little Bear had shot the cowboy, Boone. That time, Tommy had been brought in to help. He had had some tiny instruments, dressings and medicine. Crude as his old-fashioned methods were, they had worked. Omri felt poignantly the absence of an old friend, as one does—not just missing the person, but missing his skills, his role in one's life. For a moment, he felt almost angry with Tommy for being dead when he was so badly needed.

Bright Stars, who was kneeling beside Little Bear, looked up. She said something. It was some Indian word. Omri shook his head. Bright Stars wrung her hands. She pointed to the two bullet wounds, and said the word again, louder. It must be some special Indian remedy she wanted. And for the first time, Omri thought: She might be better off where she came from. She'd know what to do there.

But at least he could clean the wounds. He knew how to do that much. He had some mouthwash, horrible stuff his mother made him gargle with when he had a cold. The bottle was on his shelf. He jumped up and fetched it. His head was spinning. He was beginning to realize how insane it had been to start up with this business again; he was remembering the awful sense of responsibility, the anxiety, the unending succession of problems to be solved . . . and this time he didn't even have Patrick to give him occasional support or good ideas.

Patrick . . . But Patrick was useless. He didn't even *believe* any more.

Omri soaked a bit of the cotton from the box with the disinfectant and handed it to Bright Stars, making swabbing gestures to show her what it was for. She caught on quickly. With light, delicate strokes she cleaned the blood off Little Bear's back. No more seemed to be coming from the holes. Omri, remembering that injured people have to be kept warm, and noticing that Bright Stars was shivering, snatched up one of the gloves he'd worn to school and recklessly cut the little finger off it with some scissors. The Indian was soon inside the woollen finger, which was like a sleeping bag. Omri and Bright Stars looked at each other.

"How?" Omri asked. "How did it happen?"

Bright Stars's face grew hard. "Soldier," she said. "Fight. Gun."

"In the back?" Omri couldn't help asking. It was hard to imagine anyone as brave as Little Bear getting shot in the back.

"Fall horse," she said. "Little Bear lie. Ground. Soldiers shoot." She pointed an imaginary weapon, a rifle or a musket, gestured one, two, then waved her hand sharply to show the soldiers had run on, leaving Little Bear to die.

"You saw this?"

She nodded fiercely. "Woman see. Soldier come village. Braves fight. Soldier make fire in house. Kill many. Take prisoner. Braves chase. Out, out—far! Bright Stars hide. See Little Bear fall. See soldier—" She mimed shooting again. "Bright Stars run, catch pony, bring Little Bear home to village. All fire! Dead brave! Woman cry! I shut eyes, not see. Whoosh!" She made a strange noise like a rush of wind. Opened her eyes—and pointed at Omri with a look of acted surprise.

"And suddenly you were here."

She nodded. "Spirits bring. You save."

Omri gazed at her. He had not the very faintest idea of what to do, and here she was, trusting him.

"Don't you think you'd be better at home—in the village?" he suggested helplessly.

She shook her head violently.

"Village all fire. Dead—dead!" She pointed everywhere on the ground. "No help. Omri only help Little Bear brother."

Brother! Yes. Little Bear had swapped drops of blood with him in that last moment, making them blood brothers. He must, he must find a way to help! But how?

At that moment, Little Bear stirred and groaned.

Instantly, Bright Stars crouched beside him. Omri, whose eyes had begun to get used to focusing on minute detail once again, noticed suddenly that she had become fat. Could it be that—? But Little Bear was groaning and muttering, his legs were twitching. Omri forgot about Bright Stars's new shape for the moment.

"What's he saying?"

"Say, 'Omri, Omri,'" reported Bright Stars. There was more muttering, and then she said, "Now say, 'Brother.'" She looked up at him with a look he couldn't bear.

He stood up.

"Listen," he said hoarsely. "I have to bring help. I need—something . . ." He looked at her. "Lend me your moccasins." He pointed to her feet. Bewildered but obedient, she bent and took off the soft shoes made of bead-embroidered animal hide, and gave them to him. He wrapped them carefully in a twist of paper and put them in his pocket.

"Take care of him," he said. "I'll be back."

6

Going for Help

Omri locked his bedroom door behind him and went
downstairs.

It was Friday night (luckily, or he'd have had home-
work, which he wouldn't have been able to do). His parents
and Gillon were watching television. Adiel had gone out
with friends.

"Mum, d'you remember Patrick?" He spoke very
casually.

"Of course I remember Patrick."

"He moved to the country."

"I know."

"I saw him last week."

"Where?"

"Outside school. He said his mother had come back for a visit."

"To her sister, I expect." His mother turned back to the set.

"Her *sister*? I didn't know Patrick had an aunt!"

"Don't be silly, of course you did. She lived three doors down from our old house."

Omri frowned, remembering. "With those two revolting little girls?"

"Tamsin and Emma. Bonkins or something. Donkins. They're Patrick's cousins."

"D'you think Patrick might be *there*?"

"You can soon find out. I've still got her phone number in my book. It's on the hall table."

Three minutes later, Omri had Patrick's voice in his ear.

"Patrick? It's me. Omri. I've got to see you."

"When?"

"Tonight."

"*Tonight*?"

"It's very important."

"Can't it wait?"

Omri sensed the reluctance in Patrick's voice. He understood it. "No."

"I'm watching a horror film."

"The horror film doesn't start till eleven-thirty," Omri retorted.

41

There was a silence.

"You're not going to start up with all that rubbish about—"

"I'm coming," said Omri shortly, and rang off.

He slipped out the back door and was soon running down Hovel Road for the station.

Some of the shops, and the amusement arcade, were still open. So were the pubs. Their glass doors let out a friendly glow and lots of loud voices as Omri dashed past. In the amusement arcade the skinheads were banging away at the space invaders, not noisy and comradely like the pub-goers, but grim, intent, each bent over a machine. They didn't notice him. Omri ran swiftly on, with a feeling of relief. This horrible street was actually safer by night.

Sometimes you had to wait ages for a train, but tonight Omri was lucky, though the journey—only three stops— seemed to take forever. At the other end he began to run again, but he wasn't scared this time. He found the house of their old neighbor and rang the bell. Patrick came and stood looking at him in a far-from-welcoming way.

"Well, you'd better come in now you're here," he said.

It was a small house, just like their old one, even to the bicycles crowding the narrow hall. Omri's mother had said, only half as a joke, that the reason she'd wanted to move to the new house was so they needn't ever have bikes in the hall any more. Patrick led the way upstairs without a word, into a small back bedroom with a pair of bunk-beds, everything pink and frothy.

"My aunt makes me sleep in this pouffy girls' room," he said. "Glad I'm going home tomorrow." He sat down on the bottom bunk, leaving Omri standing. There was a brief silence. Patrick glanced up at Omri. His mouth was pinched. His eyes said, "Don't talk about it." He was silently begging Omri not to. But Omri was ruthless.

"Why are you pretending it never happened?" he asked sharply.

"What?" said Patrick. He had a sullen, stupid look, like those skinheads.

"You know what."

Patrick stared at the floor. He didn't move.

"I brought them back," said Omri.

Patrick stood up so suddenly he hit his head on the top bunk. His face had gone white. He swore under his breath. Then he said, "I don't believe you."

"I'm telling you. I put them in the cupboard and the same thing happened. It—" (he didn't like to use the word "magic," somehow) "it's still working. Just the same. Only—" Patrick was looking at him now, frowning, incredulous, as if he'd woken from a dream to find the dream was still going on. "The terrible thing is, Little Bear's been shot."

After a pause, Patrick muttered something under his breath.

Omri leaned forward. "What?"

"It's not true. None of it's true. We just . . . made it up," he half whispered.

Omri took his hand out of his pocket and held something out to Patrick. "Look. And stop kidding yourself."

Almost as if he was fighting fear, Patrick slowly looked. He blinked several times. Then he put out his hand and unwrapped the twist of paper. He stared for a long time at the tiny beaded moccasins.

"They're real," breathed Patrick.

He turned away to the window and stood looking out into the darkness. Omri let him adjust. When he turned around, he was the old Patrick again. Older, but basically unchanged.

"How did it happen?"

Omri had a mad impulse to hug him. Now at least he was not alone with it.

"Some French soldier shot him. I suppose he was French. You know the Iroquois were fighting with the English, and the French were against them. We've got to find a way to get the bullets out, or the musket balls, or whatever they are."

"Easy," said Patrick. "Get Tommy back."

Omri swallowed. "He's dead."

Patrick's mouth fell open. "*Dead?*"

"He must have been killed in the war. He said—last

time, when we were sending him back—that he could hear a big shell coming over. I bet it was the one that got him."

Patrick stared at him, aghast. "D'you mean if we hadn't sent him back at that minute—"

"I don't think that's how it works. His—his real, big body—that must've still been there, in his time, lying asleep in the trench. The shell would have killed him anyway."

Patrick pushed his hand through his hair.

"And you say Little Bear's hurt?"

"Yes. Bright Stars is with him. She thinks the spirits brought her to me to help save his life. I've got to do something. And I don't know *what*." Omri checked the shrill edge of desperation in his voice.

Patrick sat still, thinking.

"What's happened to all your old plastic people?" he asked at last. "That we used to play with."

"I think they're up in our loft."

"Mum threw mine away."

"Threw them away?" asked Omri, unbelievingly. "Without asking?"

"I hadn't played with them for ages."

"Why, anyway?"

"Look," said Patrick. "We've lost Tommy, but the magic still works. If we could find a *modern* doctor-figure, he'd be even better."

45

This disloyalty to their dead friend struck both of them at once, and Patrick flushed.

"I didn't mean . . . Tommy saved Boone's life, I know that. But we've got to be realistic. There've been a lot of advances. New drugs, new techniques. Haven't you got anyone in your collection who might—?"

Omri thought, and then shook his head.

"All mine were cowboys and knights and soldiers and stuff like that," he said.

Patrick stood up.

"But there *are* modern ones. I've seen them. I've seen them very recently." His face changed. He almost yelled: "Wait!" and rushed from the room. A few minutes later, he was back.

"Look!"

In his hand was a large, flat cardboard box of brand-new plastic figures. They weren't soldiers, or Indians. They were ordinary people from now. One look told Omri what sort. *Professional* people. There was a judge in a long wig, and several lawyers. There were businessmen with brief-cases, one in a bowler hat. There were scientists in labora-tory coats. There was a nurse. And—Omri let out a shout—there were doctors. Two of them, to be exact. One was an ordinary doctor with a stethoscope around his neck. And the other was a surgeon, in a green gown and mask.

Almost gibbering with excitement and relief—he felt as if he were looking into Aladdin's cave—Omri peered closer. The man was bent over an operating table. Yes! What Omri had been hoping for was there! Instruments—trays of them—all part of the same group! Little Bear was as good as saved!

"That's it!" he cried. "Come on, let's go!"

But, incredibly, Patrick was hesitating.

"What's *wrong*?" asked Omri impatiently.

"They're not mine."

"Oh, so what?—Whose are they?"

"My cousin's. She got them yesterday, for her birthday."

"We'll give them back!"

"Tamsin goes mad if you touch her things. She's sure to notice it's gone."

"But Little Bear may be *dying*."

Patrick gave a shrug. "Okay. Better wrap them up."

They found an old Safeways bag and dropped the whole box in. They were just going downstairs when a door opened and a girl Omri remembered only too well came out into the hall. Patrick stopped dead like a burglar caught in the act.

"Oh, God, it's her," he muttered. "See you later . . ." But he didn't turn tail. They just kept on going toward the front door.

Tamsin barred their way. She was a big girl for her age,

with a pronounced jaw and scowling brows.

"Where're *you* off to, Paddywack?" she asked taunt-ingly. She ignored Omri, although she recognized him. They'd never been precisely pally.

"I'm going out for a bit."

"Does your mum know?"

"I was just going to tell her."

"I bet."

"I was. *Excuse* me."

As he brushed past her, some possessive instinct must have warned her. She grabbed the bag. Patrick hadn't expected this, and let go of it. In a flash she had opened it and peered in. The face she raised was suddenly flushed with fury.

"You're stealing my present!" she said, slowly and men-acingly.

"No we're not! We were only borrowing it for the night."

"For the *night*! Are you crazy? I wouldn't let you borrow it for five seconds."

Something was boiling up in Omri's head. There went everything they needed to save Little Bear. That wretched girl was clutching it to her as if they were trying to part her from a bag of gold.

"We were going to ask you!" he babbled untruthfully. "Please lend them to us!"

"*No.*" Her face and voice were of stone. He knew she would never give way. An impulse born of desperation seized him. He reached out and tried to snatch the bag back from her.

She held on, and screeched. The bag tore, the box fell out and its lid came off. There on the floor lay the whole array of figures, held firmly to their backing by elastic string. Omri didn't hesitate. He simply fell on top of them, his fingers under him, clutching and wrenching. Tamsin fell on top of him, clutching and wrenching *him*. He felt his ear being wrung half off, his head being pounded, and his ankle kicked, sharp as a dog bite, by Tamsin's pointed shoe. As they writhed, first one bicycle and then a second crashed down on top of them.

A moment later a door slammed and an exasperated adult voice roared:

"Have you kids gone mad? Stop it this instant! *Tamsin*—!"

She and the tangle of bikes were hiked bodily off him, putting a stop to the immediate torture, though aches lingered.

"They're nicking my present! They're nicking my models!" shrieked the dangling Tamsin, threshing all her limbs in the air like a monstrous spider.

"*Patrick?*"

But Patrick was already at the front door and Omri was scrambling to his feet.

"We don't want her models," he muttered. "It was only a joke!" And before more could be said, they were outside.

Patrick's mother appeared in the doorway, crying after them: "Where do you boys think you're going?"

Patrick yelled back, "I'm sleeping over at Omri's!"

"Come back!" called his mother. "You haven't got your toothbru-u-ush!" But they were already around the corner.

7

Matron

UNDER THE FIRST STREETLAMP, Omri pulled up. His heart was hammering.

"Well?" asked Patrick eagerly. "Did you get it? Let's look!"

Omri had *something* in his hand. But he knew it wasn't the one he'd wanted. It wasn't the surgeon—he would have been able to feel the square shape of the operating table. It was a single figure. He held his hand closed around it, afraid to look. What if it was only a lawyer or that idiotic bowler-hatted businessman?

Slowly, in an agony of suspense, Omri uncurled his fingers. Both boys slumped with despair. Omri gave a deep groan.

Then Patrick rallied.

"It could be worse. Nurses have to know *some*thing."

"They can't operate. They're not trained."

"It's better than nothing."

They walked on, Omri sunk in gloom. Patrick kept trying to cheer him up.

"Listen. If he can hang on till tomorrow, we can go out and buy anything we like. At the model shop they'll have the same set. Meanwhile at least the nurse will be able to tell us how bad he is."

"If she doesn't drop dead when we bring her out of the cupboard," said Omri. He was cursing himself for not managing to grab the surgeon. He would also, incidentally, have liked to jump up and down on Tamsin's stomach until she burst like a balloon. He was bruised all over.

Patrick of course had never seen the district where Omri now lived. As they came out of the station, he paused, glanced down Hovel Road and said, "Blimey. This is a bit rough."

Omri said nothing. They began to hurry towards his house.

"What are the kids like around here?"

"Well. You have to stand up for yourself."

They were passing the amusement arcade—on the other side of the street, of course. It was just closing. The proprietor, a surly-looking Sikh, was urging everyone out.

There was a good deal of swearing, jeering and shoving. A scuffle started. A rather small skinhead jostled an older boy, who reacted by hurling him unceremoniously into the road, where he was narrowly missed by a passing car.

"Crumbs!" exclaimed Patrick. "Did you see that?"

"Yes, and it'll be us next if they spot us," said Omri. "Come on!"

Omri's mother opened the door to his knock. She was furious.

"Where on earth have you been? Don't you ever go out again at night without telling me—I've been frantic! Oh. Hallo, Patrick, fancy seeing you. Are you planning to spend the night?"

Patrick looked daunted, but Omri had no time to pacify his mother. After a brief "Sorry, Mum!" he dragged Patrick after him up the stairs, deaf to her enquiries about where he'd been and where Patrick would sleep.

As soon as they had the door of his bedroom shut behind them, Omri switched on the main light. He'd left his bedside lamp on so Bright Stars wouldn't be in the dark. Patrick cautiously approached the chest, his eyes wide, as if his unbelief had come back to him, and the sight of the living miniature people struck him afresh as incredible. Bright Stars had jumped to her feet as they came in. She recognized Patrick at once and raised her hand to greet him.

"Hallo, Bright Stars," he said softly. "How's Little Bear?"

She stepped aside and pointed. Little Bear's eyes were open. They were big with pain. He fastened them on Patrick, and then saw Omri. He didn't speak, but a look of joy came over his face. He closed his eyes.

"Omri help now?" asked Bright Stars beseechingly.

"We're going to try." He wanted to tell her not to be too hopeful, but he couldn't. He brought the figure of the nurse out of his pocket. He and Patrick examined it again.

"She's wearing one of those weird high hats," said Patrick. "When I was in hospital having my tonsils out, nurses with those sort of hats were important. All the others scurried about when they came into the ward."

"Maybe she's a matron?" said Omri, who though he hadn't ever been in a hospital, did not watch TV for nothing.

"Yeah, something like that. Come on, let's do it."

No matter what the circumstances, this was always a thrilling moment. Into the cupboard went the little female figure in its blue uniform dress and white apron and elaborate cap. Would she be old or young? Awful or nice? Above all, how would she react when she saw them?

In the past the little people they had brought to life had been superstitious enough, or drunk enough, to accept the fantastic situation. Even Tommy had been easy to convince that he was dreaming. But a modern person might have much more trouble accepting the facts.

A quick turn back and forth of the key, and instantly a

severe voice could be heard calling from inside the cupboard:

"Nurse! NURSE! Phone through immediately and tell
Maintenance there's been a power cut in Ward 12! No need
for alarm, ladies, just a little electrical failure; we'll have the
emergency generator working in no time!"

Omri opened the cupboard door.

"Ah!" cried the voice. "*That's* more like it! Now, what
was I—"

And it stopped.

Omri swung the door right back. The matron stood
there on the shelf where they had put her, her hands
coming slowly away from her hips. She looked at the two
enormous faces for a few seconds. Then she covered her
eyes, rubbed them, shook her head briskly, and looked
again. Then she said, "What's this, then, boys, some kind of
trick? Put the mirrors away and get back to your beds."
Then, when nothing happened, her face suddenly went as
white as her cap. She did a kind of spin on one heel and fell
straight backwards off the shelf.

Omri just managed to catch her. He'd been half expecting something of the sort. She lay in the palm of his hand
in a dead faint. Omri marveled at the feeling of her tiny
warm limp body, in its crisp starched clothes, alive . . . He
transported her gently to the chest and showed her to
Bright Stars.

"White woman dead?" she asked, aghast.

"No, no. She's just had a fright. Make her sit up and put her head between her knees." He showed her how. Bright Stars wasted no time. After a minute or two, the matron showed signs of reviving. The first thing she did was reach up to check that her cap, which was like a white organdy castle with flying buttresses and banners, was still in place. Miraculously, it was.

She scrambled to her feet and stared around her. She was middle-aged, Omri guessed from her face and voice. She wore glasses and no makeup and looked formidable. He was glad that he was not a patient in her charge. At the same time, she did look as if she knew her job—if only she was not too terrified to do it.

He cleared his throat.

"I know it's hard to believe," he began, "but you've come through a magic cupboard which has made you very small. Please don't be frightened. You can think it's a dream if you like, or some kind of trick, but there's nothing to be afraid of. After you've helped us, you can go back to your . . . your normal life. Would you mind telling us your name?"

The woman opened and shut her mouth several times like a goldfish. Then she managed to say, very faintly, "You may call me Matron." Then she swayed and put her hand to her forehead. "I must be going mad!" she muttered. And she looked as if she might fall over again.

"Please! You're not mad. Don't faint!"

Matron stiffened at once and lifted her chin.

"*Faint? Me?* Don't be absurd, I've never fainted in my entire life!" She straightened her splendid cap and stared at them haughtily. "Matrons don't faint! The very idea."

Patrick opened his mouth, but Omri nudged him into silence.

"I beg your pardon," he said.

"Not that I wouldn't be grateful for a strong cup of tea," she remarked severely. "Especially if there's any work to be done."

"There is!" Omri exclaimed eagerly. "I'll get you some tea later, but could you please look at a patient for us?"

Bright Stars was already almost pulling Matron over to where Little Bear was lying on the ground.

"Dear me," murmured the Matron. She adjusted her cap and her glasses and knelt down beside Little Bear's prone form. After a brief but efficient examination, she rose, looked over her glasses at Bright Stars, evidently decided *she* was innocent of any crime, and turned her accusing gaze on the boys.

"This man," she announced, "has been shot in the back."

"Yes, we know," said Omri.

"He needs an immediate operation to remove the bullets."

"We *know*," said Omri. "Only, they're not bullets, they're musket balls. You see—"

"He must be taken at once to the nearest hospital. I recommend my own—St. Thomas's."

"Matron," said Patrick.

"Yes, young man?"

"We can't. You see, St. Thomas's is our size, and he is your size. They wouldn't be able to help him. Everything would be too big for him. Don't you see?"

Matron closed her eyes for a moment, swayed visibly (Omri stretched out a hand to catch her) and then righted herself with an effort.

"This is exceedingly peculiar," she said, "to say the very least. I don't profess to understand what has happened to me. But still . . . press on! What do you suggest?"

"Could he hold out until tomorrow?"

She pursed her lips and shook her head. "Most unwise."

Omri's heart sank. "Couldn't—couldn't *you* do it?"

The Matron started violently. "*I*—? Perform the task of a surgeon? Such a thing would be unthinkable. The etiquette of the medical profession absolutely forbids it."

"But if it didn't?"

"What do you mean?"

"I mean—*could* you do it, if you were allowed to?"

"'Allowed to'! It is not a matter of permission."

"Well, then?—You see," Omri said, and now the same imploring note crept into his voice as had been in Bright Stars's eyes, "there's no one else."

Matron turned and stared down at Little Bear for a long moment.

"But I have no equipment," she said at last.

Patrick threw back his head with a groan. "That's true . . . Of course! No one can operate without instruments! Why didn't we think of that?"

"I did think of it," said Omri. "We've got instruments. Sort of."

Patrick turned to gape at him. "Where?"

For answer, Omri reached again for the plastic figure which had once been Tommy. Silently he put him back into the cupboard and turned the key. When he opened the door, there once again was the neat pile of clothes, the boots—and the bag with the red cross on it.

8

The Operation

"**Y**OU'RE *BRILLIANT*," breathed Patrick as Omri delicately picked up the tiny object. With his free hand he overturned one of the boxes in which the plastic figures had been stored, spread Kleenex on it, and set the bag in the middle.

Matron bustled over with a swish of starched apron. She started a little at the sight of the battered old bag, but not half as much as she did when she opened it. She fairly reeled back.

"Are you seriously suggesting that I pull bullets out of a man's back with this antiquated collection of museum pieces!" she almost shrieked.

"Are they so very different from what you use today?"

asked Omri desperately.

Matron gingerly plucked a tiny hypodermic syringe from the bag and held it up like a dead rat between finger and thumb.

"Look at it! Just look! I ask you!"

"Matron," Omri said earnestly. "You don't seem to understand. *That's all there is.* It's the best we can manage. If you can't do it, he'll die. Our friend. Please! All we ask is that you try."

Matron gave Omri an enigmatic look. Then she took hold of Tommy's bag and briskly emptied it on the padded table. All sorts of microscopic things came out. The boys could just make out the rolls of bandages, dressings, dark bottles, and instruments packed in flat cases. She examined these very minutely and then straightened up and said, "Of course this is some kind of nightmare. But even in nightmares, it is my policy to do my best."

Omri and Patrick clutched each other.

"You mean, you'll do it?"

"If you can provide me with an operating table, a bright light, some disinfectant, and a strong cup of tea."

Omri could, and did, provide all those things. By this time it was one o'clock in the morning and the whole household was fast asleep, but he tiptoed downstairs and fetched disinfectant, cotton, some clean handkerchiefs, and an electric kettleful of boiling water. He also detached the cap from a tube of toothpaste and washed it out. That was for a mug. Then he made some strong tea with a tea bag and added milk and sugar. He hoped she took sugar. He carried all this on a tray up the stairs very quietly.

When he returned to his room, Patrick had fixed up the box as an operating table. Omri's bedside lamp, which had a flexible neck and a 100-watt bulb—his mother had a thing about reading in a bad light—had been moved onto the chest. The light shone straight down onto the table, making no shadows. There was Kleenex spread everywhere. It looked very hygienic. Little Bear had already been laid on the table, and Matron, armed with a tiny pair of scissors, was soon cutting up a handkerchief to make a surgical gown for herself and an operating sheet for Little Bear.

"I shall need an assistant," she said briskly. "What about the Indian girl?"

"She doesn't speak much English."

"We'll see. She looks bright enough." She beckoned Bright Stars, who was already at her elbow. "How!" she said in a loud voice. Bright Stars looked puzzled. "When I point—you give," Matron went on. Bright Stars nodded intently.

"You say. I do."

Omri was directed to pour a drop of disinfectant and some of the boiling water into a small tin lid Patrick had prized off a box of candy-drops. The water turned white.

Matron dropped the instruments in, and after some moments, poured off the liquid into another lid. Meanwhile, Omri was dipping up a few drops of tea into the toothpaste cap.

"Ah! Thank you, dear," she said when she saw it. She seemed quite cheerful now. She picked up the cap in both hands. It was, to her, almost the size of a bucket, but she drank most of it at one go, and smacked her lips. "That's more like it! What spinach is to Popeye, tea is to me! Now then, let's get on with it."

The boys saw very little of the operation itself. The light shone straight down on the white-covered table. Matron stood with her back to them, working silently. Every now and then she would point at something on the tray. Bright Stars would swiftly pick it up and hand it to her. Only once or twice did she fumble, and then Matron would snap her fingers impatiently. For a long time there was not a sound except the occasional stamp of the pony's foot or the clink of metal.

Then Matron said, "I do believe we're in luck."

The boys, who had been afraid to come too close, though Matron had made them both tie handkerchiefs around their faces, leaned forward.

"One—er—ball went in one side and straight out the other. Missed his lung by a hairbreadth, I'm thankful to say. I've patched that up as best I could. Now I'm playing hide-

and-seek with the other one. I think it's lodged against his shoulder blade. Not far in. I . . . think . . . I've . . . got it. Yes!" She made a sharp movement and then held up a minute pair of tweezers. Whatever they held was far too small to see, but the tips were red and Omri shuddered. Matron dropped the bit of metal into the tray with a ping. Suddenly she began to laugh.

"Whatever would St. Thomas's surgical staff say if they could see me now!" she gurgled.

"Will he be okay?" Omri asked breathlessly.

"Oh, I think so! Yes, indeed! He's a very lucky lad, is your Indian friend."

"We're all lucky to have found you," said Omri sincerely.

Matron was stripping the wrapper off a large field dressing. "First World War dressings," she was murmuring. "Amazing how they've lasted! As if they were made last week!"

She indicated to Bright Stars that she should help her apply it to Little Bear's back. Then they bandaged him between them, and after that she wiped her perspiring face on a scrap of cotton.

"You can turn the light off now," she said. "Phew! I'm hot." Her towering cap was collapsing like an ice palace, but she didn't seem to care. "Any more tea?—What an experience! Wouldn't have missed it for the world. Always thought I could do simple ops as well as any of those fat cats . . . Oh dear, what *am* I saying?" And she chuckled again at her own disrespect to professional etiquette.

After swigging down another bucket of tea and making sure Bright Stars had some too, she checked Little Bear's pulse, gave Bright Stars some simple instructions, and then said, "Gentlemen, I think, if you don't mind, I'd better be getting back to St. Thomas's. Goodness alone knows how they're coping without me! I'm afraid the unthinkable has happened and I have fallen asleep on duty . . . I will simply never live it down."

She shook hands with Bright Stars, and then gave her a pat—not on her shoulder, oddly, but on her stomach.

"Take care of your husband," she said. "And take care of yourself, too." Bright Stars looked shy. "You'll have a nice surprise for him if he doesn't come to very soon!" Then she waved to the boys, straightened her wilted cap and, hiking up her skirt over her black stockings, clambered back into the cupboard.

When she'd gone, Omri watched Bright Stars settling down at Little Bear's side. He was still lying on the "table," warmly wrapped up and sleeping soundly.

"What did she mean about a surprise?" he asked Patrick, who was yawning hugely.

"Oh, come on! Didn't you notice?"

"Notice what?"

"Her big belly. She's going to have a baby."

"A baby! Wow! That'd be great!"

"Are you nuts? That's all we need!"

"Indian women manage by themselves," said Omri, who'd read about it. "They don't make any fuss. Not like our mothers."

"I should think any mother'd make a fuss if she had to have you," said Patrick. "Where do I kip?"

Omri was beginning to feel exhausted too, but it seemed heartless to go to sleep.

"Do you think we should?"

"She said he'd be quite okay. She told Bright Stars what to do. There's not much we can do, anyway. Look, can I just put these cushions on the floor? I'm knackered."

In three minutes he was flat out.

It took Omri a little longer. He crouched by the chest and stared at Little Bear and Bright Stars. She must be tired too, especially considering . . .

"Do you need anything, Bright Stars? Something to eat?"

She raised her tired eyes to him and gave a little nod.

"I'll get you something!" he whispered.

Down he went once again. He didn't turn on lights this time. The reflection from the kitchen light could be seen in his parents' bedroom. He had no desire to explain to anyone what he was doing up at such an hour. The light from the streetlamp was enough to show him cake, bread, butter—

What was that?

Something had gone past the window. He'd seen it out of the corner of his eye. He froze. He could have sworn it was a man's head. When he could unfreeze, he went to the window and looked out.

All he could see was Kitsa sitting on the sill. Which would have settled the matter, except for one thing. Her head was up, her ears were pricked—and not at Omri, but in the other direction.

Omri climbed the stairs with the food, feeling more than a little uneasy. It seemed to him, on reflection, that the head he had seen had shone in the streetlamp as if it had no hair.

9

A Good Luck Piece

LITTLE BEAR'S RECOVERY was little short of miraculous. The operation was a complete success. By the next day he was sitting up, demanding food and other services, not particularly grateful for his deliverance and, in general, very much himself as Omri remembered him.

He was unable to hide his delight at seeing Omri again. He tried to conceal his feelings behind a mask of dignity, but through his wooden expression his black eyes gleamed and a grin kept twitching at his stern mouth.

"Omri grow much," he remarked between slurps of a mug of hot instant soup. (There was a distinct shortage of toothpaste tops throughout the house, which Omri's

68

mother was to remark on.) "But still only boy. Not chief, like Little Bear."

"Are you a real chief now?" Omri asked. He was sitting on the floor beside the chest, gazing in rapture at his little Indian, restored to him, and, almost, to health.

Little Bear nodded impressively. "Father die. Little Bear chief of tribe."

Omri glanced at Bright Stars. How much had she told him of the tragedy which had overtaken their village? She seemed to understand his thought and signaled him quickly behind Little Bear's back. Omri nodded. Much better not to say too much until Little Bear was stronger. He hadn't asked any questions yet.

Patrick had stayed for breakfast and then, reluctantly, phoned his mother. He came back up to Omri's room looking bleak.

"She says I've got to come back," he said. "We're leaving today. I asked if I could stay and come back later, but she said I have to leave here in an hour."

Omri didn't say anything. He didn't see how Patrick could bear to leave. To make matters worse, Omri's parents had particularly asked if he could stay over another night. They were going to a party that evening and would be home late. Adiel and Gillon would be out too. There'd be a baby-sitter of course, but she was a stodgy old lady, and

Patrick would be company for Omri. Omri thought Patrick's mother was being entirely unreasonable, and said so. Patrick was inclined to agree.

Meanwhile, they had this hour. They decided to spend it talking and doing things for the Indians. The first thing Little Bear asked for was his old longhouse, built by himself when he'd been with Omri last year. Fortunately, Omri still had it, or what was left of it. It had been made on a seed tray packed with earth, but this had dried out in the interval, so that several of the upright posts had come adrift and some of the bark tiles, so carefully shaped by Little Bear and hung on the crosspieces, had shriveled and dropped off.

When Little Bear saw his derelict masterwork he had to be forcibly restrained from leaping out of bed immediately to repair it.

"How Omri let fall down? Why Omri not mend?" he shouted wrathfully.

Omri knew better than to argue.

"I couldn't do it like you can," he said. "My fingers are too big."

"Too big!" agreed Little Bear darkly. He stared at the longhouse from his bed. Omri had spent the early hours, before anyone was awake, making him a better bed from two matchboxes, giving him a headboard to sit up against. His mind was roving in all directions, thinking of ways to make Little Bear and Bright Stars more comfortable. He still had the old tepee . . . As soon as the Indian was a bit better, he would probably prefer to use that, for privacy. Omri had fixed a ramp leading onto the seed tray, and Bright Stars had begun to go up and down it carrying bedding into the tepee, like a little bird making its nest. A fat little bird . . . Omri wondered, watching her stagger to and fro, how long it would be before her baby came.

He was busy giving her a water supply. It was a sort of pond. The container was the lid of a coffee jar, sunk into the earth of the seed tray near the tepee. He was now making a proper bucket out of one of the toothpaste caps, by piercing two holes in the sides with a needle heated red-hot in the flame of an old candle he'd found, and threading in a handle made from a bit of one of his mother's fine hair-pins. That would make it easier to carry. Of course, that was just the beginning of all the things that would be needed if they stayed long.

Bright Stars vanished into the tepee, and Little Bear, who had been watching her too, beckoned Omri closer.

"Soon I father!" he said proudly, and hit himself on the chest. A flash of pain crossed his face.

"Yes," said Omri, "so you'd better rest up and get well."

"I well!" He shifted restlessly about on the matchbox bed. Suddenly he said: "Where other brother?"

"What do you mean—my brothers?"

"No! Little Bear brother! Blood brother, like Omri."

It occurred to Omri and Patrick at the same moment whom he meant.

Patrick had also been busy. He had gone outside earlier and dug up a very small turf of grass from the garden—a piece of living lawn about six inches square, a paddock for the pony to graze on. It was to have a fence around it, which Patrick was making out of twigs, string and glue. Now he looked up from this with an unreadable look on his face.

"When your mum threw your models away—" began Omri slowly.

"Yeah?"

"Did she get rid of . . . all of them?"

"As far as I know."

"You really are the *pits*," said Omri between his teeth.

"Me? Why?"

"I suppose you just threw him in with the others and left him for your mum to chuck in the dustbin!"

"What are you talking about?"

"You know darn well! *Boone.*"

Patrick dropped his eyes. Omri couldn't tell what he felt. He seemed almost to be smiling, but Omri felt suddenly so furious with him that this only made him angrier.

Though they had spoken quietly, Little Bear's sharp ears had caught the gist.

"Who throw Boone? I want! Want see blood brother! Who throw, I kill!" he roared.

Bright Stars emerged from the tepee at the first roar and darted to his side. She forced him to lie on his back and pinioned him to the bed by main force until he calmed down a little and evidently promised her to behave. Then she hurried to the edge of the chest with a gleam in her eyes that boded no good at all.

"Where Little Bear brother?" she demanded. "Little Bear want! No good him get angry! Omri bring Boone. Now."

Omri's insides seemed to be churning up with an anger no less strong than the Indian's. He turned on Patrick.

"You must have been mad to let your mother throw him away! Just because for some idiotic reason you wanted to pretend none of it ever happened! I'm going to kick your head in, you dim wally!" And he made a move towards Patrick.

Patrick didn't step back. He stood with his hand in his pocket.

"He's here," he said.

Omri stopped short, jolted as if he'd stepped up a nonexistent step. "What—?"

"He's here. In my pocket."

Slowly he withdrew his hand and opened it. Lying in the palm was the crying cowboy, on his white horse.

Boone!—as large as life. Or rather, as small.

Omri uttered a shout of joy.

"You've got him! You had him all the time!" Then his grin faded. "Are you mad? Why didn't you say so in the first place?"

"I'm not exactly proud of the fact that I still carry him everywhere," Patrick said.

"So you hadn't stopped believing?"

"I don't know. I wanted to. I tried to tell my brother about it once, and he teased me for a solid week, saying I was a nut case, telling everyone I believed in fairies. It really got me. Of course I couldn't prove a thing, not even to myself. So I decided it never happened. But I . . . I just kept Boone in my pocket all the time, like . . . well, sort of for good luck."

Omri had picked up the figure of Boone tenderly and was examining it. The horse's legs had become a bit bent, and Boone's beloved hat was looking decidedly the worse for wear. But it was still, unmistakably, even in plastic, Boone. It was the way they had last seen him, sitting on his horse, in his ten-gallon hat, his hand holding a big red bandanna to his nose, blowing a trumpet blast of farewell.

"Ah cain't stand sayin' good-bye. Ah jest re-fuse t' say it, that's all! Ah'll only bust out cryin' if Ah do . . ."

"Come on, Boone!" whispered Omri. And he put him, without more ado, into the cupboard and turned the key.

74

He and Patrick bent over eagerly, bumping heads. Neither of them brought to the surface of his mind the deep fear they shared. Boone, too, had lived in dangerous times. Omri knew now that time worked the same at both ends, so to speak. A year had passed for him, and, in another place and time, a year had passed for his little men. And an awful lot (and a lot of it awful!) could happen in a year.

But almost at once their fears were laid to rest. There was a split second's silence, and then, on the other side of the cupboard door, Boone began battering and kicking it, and a faint stream of swear words issued through the metal.

"Ah ain't puttin' up with it! No, sir, it ain't fair, it ain't dawggone well right! Ah ain't bin drinkin', Ah ain't bin fightin', Ah ain't cheated at poker in over a week! Ain't no law kin sling a man in jail when he's inny-cint as a nooborn babe, never mind keepin' him shut in a cell so dark he cain't see his own mus-tash!"

The boys were too fascinated to do anything at first, even open the door. They just crouched there, grinning imbecilically at each other.

"It's Boone! It's really him!" breathed Patrick.

But Boone, all unaware, and getting no response to his yells and blows, now decided no one was listening, and his voice began to quaver.

"They done up and left me," he muttered. "Gone

plumb away and left ol' Boone alone in the dark . . ." There was a pause, followed by a long nose-blow that shook the cupboard. "T'ain't fu-funny," he went on, his voice now definitely shaking with sobs. "Don't they know a man kin be brave as a lion and still skeered o' the dark? Ain't they got no 'magination, leavin' a fella ter rot in this pitch-black hell-hole? . . ." His voice rose on a shrill tide of tearful complaint.

Omri could not bear it a second longer. He opened the door. The light struck through and Boone instantly looked up, his red bandanna dropping to the floor between his knees. He jumped to his feet, staring, his mouth agape, his battered old hat askew on his ginger head. The horse backed off and snorted.

"Well, Ah'll be e-ternally hornswoggled!" Boone got out at last. "If it ain't you-all!"

10

Boone's Brain Wave

"YES, IT'S US-ALL!—I mean, it's us!" said Patrick excitedly. He capered about, stiff-legged, unable to contain himself.

Omri, too, was over the moon. "It's so good to see you, Boone," he cried, wishing he could wring the little man's hand and bang him on the back.

Boone, who must have fallen off his horse at some point, now scrambled to his feet and dusted himself off. The horse came up behind him in the cupboard and nudged him forcefully in the back, as if to say, "I'm here too." Omri could just about stroke its tiny nose with the tip of his little finger. The horse bunted it, nodding its head up and down, and then exchanged whinnies with Little Bear's pony on the distant seed tray.

"And it's mighty good t'see you fellas!" Boone was saying warmly, as he scrambled out of the cupboard. "Bin more'n a mite dull without mah hallucy-nations . . . Wal! Waddaya know, if it ain't the li'l Injun gal!" Bright Stars had taken a few steps toward him timidly. He raised his hat. "Howdy, Injun lady! Hey, but whur's th' other one? That redskin that made me his blood brother—after he'd half killed me?" He looked around the top of the chest, but Little Bear's matchbox bed had its back to him. "Tarnation take me if'n Ah didn't miss that dawggone varmint when Ah woke up that last time . . . Or 'went back,' or whatever ya call it . . ." He rubbed his shirt front reminiscently. "Mah ol' pals thought Ah'd gawn plumb loco when Ah tried t' tell 'em how Ah got my wound!"

"Are you okay now, Boone?"

"Me? Ah'm jest fine! Y' cain't kill Boo-hoo Boone s' easy, even if'n he does look a mite soft. So whur's Li'l Bear? Lemme shake the hand that shot me, t' show thur ain't no hard feelin's!"

Bright Stars didn't understand much of this, but she heard Little Bear's name. She took Boone by the arm and drew him over to the bed. When Boone saw the prostrate figure of the Indian he stopped short.

"Holy smoke, whut happened t' him?"

"He got shot too. By Frenchmen," Omri added in a low

voice, and signaled to Boone not to ask questions. But Boone was not the most tactful of men.

"Jee-hoshaphat! Never did trust them Frenchies. Got one runnin' our saloon. Someday someone's gonna run *him* . . . right outa town! Waters the whiskey, y' know," he added confidentially to Bright Stars.

At the word "whiskey," Little Bear opened his eyes (he had dropped off to sleep) and tried to sit up. When he saw Boone bending over him he let out a cry of recognition, and then fell back again with a hand to his bandaged chest.

"Gee, the pore ol' savage!" said Boone, shaking his head. He sniffed. "Not that he probably didn't deserve it, they're allus up to no good, but all th' same Ah cain't stand to see a man in pain."

He wiped away a tear.

"He's much better now," said Patrick. "There's nothing to start crying about."

Boone blew his nose loudly and plonked himself down on the bed.

"Tell me th' whole thing," he said.

"Not now," said Omri hurriedly.

"Why'n thunder not? Ah gotta hear sometime. C'mon, Injun. Or are ya ashamed o' somethin' ya done to that Frenchie t' make him take a shot at ya?"

Little Bear lay on the bed and stared up at Boone. There was suddenly tension in the air as they all—Bright Stars, too—waited for him to remember . . . to ask.

Slowly he raised himself onto his elbows. His eyes had gone narrow, his face taut and scowling. Suddenly he opened his eyes wide and let out a wild cry. "Aaiiiiii!"

Bright Stars put her hands to her face, turned and fled up the ramp and into the tepee.

"Whut got into her?" Boone asked, looking after her, puzzled.

But another anguished cry transfixed them all.

"Little Bear remember! Soldiers come—burn village! Burn corn! Many . . . many . . ." He opened and closed his hands rapidly, holding up ten fingers again and again. "Iroquois braves fight—but not enough—not got guns— horses . . . Enemy break—burn—steal—kill . . . kill . . ."

His voice cracked. He stopped speaking.

Another man might have broken down and wept. But Little Bear just stared, wild-eyed and frozen-faced. His mouth was shut in a straight line, like a knife-cut in his hard face. Only his hands quivered at his sides, and his fingers became hooks.

"Gee whiz, fella," muttered Boone at last. "That's too bad."

There was a long silence. Nobody moved. Little Bear lay on his back, his eyes open. He seemed to be neither fully awake, nor asleep. Omri passed a finger back and forth in front of those staring eyes—they didn't respond.

Omri, Patrick and Boone looked anxiously at each other.

"What shall we do?"

"Nuthin'," said Boone. "Pore guy's had a shock. Happened t' me once't. Came to after Ah got knocked out in some kinda ruckus . . . couldn't remember a thing. Started in talkin' and drinkin' jes like ever'thin' was normal, when all of a sudden, it come back t' me. *A lynchin'*. A mob of coyotes just strung a fella up for somethin' he didn't even do. Most horriblest thing Ah ever saw. Ah jest laid there, seein't it all over agin. Took me a danged long time t' git over it. An' that wasn't s' bad, neither, as what he's a-seein' now, pore critter . . ."

Tears of sympathy were streaming down the cowboy's leathery cheeks.

"Them rotten Frenchies . . . Mixin' in . . . Sneakin' up on 'em that-a-way an' skeerin' thur wimmenfolk an' all. Gee. Ah sure would like to help them pore folk, if'n it hadn't a happened s' long ago!"

This showed an extraordinary change of heart for Boone, who had been absolutely down on Indians when they'd first known him. Omri said, "If we sent them back now, it would be all still going on. If you wanted to help, maybe we could send you back to their time—if Little Bear just held on to you, you'd all go back together."

Boone, who had had his face buried in his red bandanna, froze for a moment. His eyes slowly appeared above the red spotted cloth.

"Me?" he said in a quavering voice.

"Well, you said you'd like to help. You've got a gun, after all. And you don't like Frenchmen. Maybe you'd like to shoot a few of them—"

"—Before they shoot me!" finished Boone. "That's a great idee, thanks a lot. Things is tough and dangerous enough whur Ah come from, Ah mean, *when* Ah come from, without goin' back a hundred years t' when things wuz ten times worse. Come t' that . . . what's stoppin' *you* from lendin' a hand t' the redskins if'n yer s' crazy about 'em?"

Patrick and Omri looked at each other, startled.

"We can't go back!" Patrick exclaimed. "How could we? We can't fit into the cupboard!"

Boone looked at them, looked consideringly at the small bathroom cabinet, less than a foot high, and then back at the boys again.

"That's true," he said grudgingly. "Ah reckon Ah cain't argue 'bout that. But thur's still a way Ah kin think of, that ya could help 'em, if'n you'd a mind ter."

"How?" they asked at once.

"What's that, down over yonder? It's s' danged far away, Ah cain't see properly, but it looks to me like a whole bunch o' folks layin' in a heap in a box."

The boys looked where he was pointing. Down on the floor was the biscuit tin full of Omri's collection of plastic figures. He'd gone up to the loft that morning to fetch it. Now he lifted it and put it on the chest, the top of which was now getting rather crowded.

"Lift me up and lemme look," ordered the little man.

Patrick put his hand down close to him. Boone heaved himself onto it as if he were scrambling onto a horse without a saddle. Patrick "flew" him over the box. He lay down flat and peered over the side of Patrick's hand, hanging on to his precious hat.

"Lookit that! Whatcha think ya got down there, if'n it ain't all kindsa men with all kindsa shootin' irons? If'n you could stick 'em all in the cupboard and bring 'em to life and then send 'em back with the Injuns, they'd come out th' other end and send them Frenchies scooting back to France as fast as greased lightnin'!"

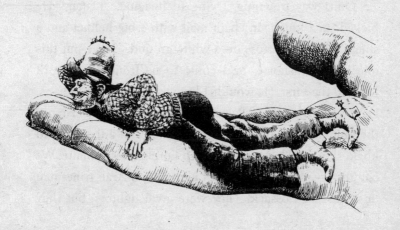

Omri and Patrick looked at each other.

"Would it work?" breathed Patrick, his eyes alight.

Omri could see that it was not just the possibility of helping the Indians that was getting him excited. From the very beginning, Patrick had wanted to experiment with the cupboard. Omri had barely been able to prevent him from stuffing dozens of soldiers in, bringing whole armies to life and making them fight . . . This looked like just the excuse he'd been wanting.

The idea had a strong appeal for Omri, too. But he was more cautious.

"We'd have to think about it," he said.

Patrick almost slammed his hand, with Boone on it, down again on the chest.

"You're always *thinking*!" he said disgustedly. "Why don't we just try it?"

Omri was frowning, trying to imagine. "Listen." He picked up a knight in chain mail with a big helmet and a shield with a red cross on a white ground. "If we put this one in, for instance, he'd come to us from the time of Richard the First. He wouldn't know a thing about Indians. He'd want to go off to Palestine and kill Saracens." He put the knight down and picked up a soldier in a flat cap and khaki shorts. "This one's a French Foreign Legionnaire. We couldn't even talk to him. Let alone to an Arab tribesman or a Russian Cossack. They were great fighters, but they wouldn't just agree to be in an army fighting Frenchmen in America on the side of the Indians. They're not *toys*. Every one of them's a person—I mean, if we brought them to life. We'd have to explain everything, half of them wouldn't believe it, others might think they'd gone crazy—"

But Patrick interrupted in high impatience. "Oh, what are you on about? Who's talking about soldiers with swords and axes and old-fashioned popguns? What about *these*?"

He dug his hand into the tin and came up with a fistful of British soldiers. Some had self-loading rifles, others had submachine guns. There was a howitzer, a 37-mm. anti-tank gun, three rocket launchers, and a variety of grenades. Omri stared at the firepower bristling out between Patrick's fingers. They had an army there, all right!

Patrick was already moving toward the cupboard, the handful of soldiers ready to thrust in.

"No," said Omri, as he had once before. "Stop!"

"I'm going to do it!" said Patrick.

Just at that moment, they heard footsteps coming up the stairs.

As one, they turned and sat on the very edge of the chest, facing the door, forming a human screen.

Omri's mother put her head in.

"Patrick, your mother just rang. Your cousin Tamsin has had a nasty fall off her bicycle and your mother's going to stay and help your aunt, so you won't be going home today."

Patrick's face lit up. "Great! That means I can stay the night here!"

"I'm sorry about your poor cousin."

"I'm not," said Patrick promptly. "I hope she broke a leg."

"Really, Patrick! That's not nice."

"Nor is she," said Patrick feelingly.

Omri's mother was looking at them curiously. "You do look odd, sitting there like Tweedledum and Tweedledee," she said. "Are you hiding something from me?"

"Yes," said Omri. It was always better to be quite frank with his parents if possible. Luckily they didn't expect to be in on everything he did.

"Oh, well," she said, "I hope it's nothing too awful. There'll be a bite of lunch in a little while. I'll call you."

And she went off.

Patrick slumped with relief. "She's just not normal, your mum," he muttered. "Mine wouldn't have rested till she'd had a good look . . ." He brought his hand from behind his back and opened it and looked at the soldiers. The uncontrollable impulse to put them in the cupboard had subsided, but he still wanted to very badly. Omri could see that.

11

Target Omri!

BRIGHT STARS WAS calling them.

She had come to Little Bear's bedside again and was now helping him to struggle into a sitting position.

"I don't think he should sit up yet," said Omri anxiously. "Not—sit—up." Bright Stars looked very worried, but Little Bear brushed her aside, gritting his teeth.

"Little Bear sit. Stand. Go back and fight!"

"No. You can't. You're not strong enough."

"I strong enough! I chief. Chief not sit in far place when tribe in trouble! Omri put in box. Omri send back! Chief Little Bear say."

But Omri was adamant. "You're not going anywhere till you're better."

He looked into the Indian's face. He understood very well how he must be feeling. Like a deserter, even though his getting shot, and being here, were no fault of his own at all.

Once, Omri had been away on a week's school trip and when he got back he found that while he'd been gone, his mother, alone in the house, had cut herself very badly on a broken bottle. With her hand pouring blood she had managed to get to the phone, an ambulance had come and she was soon in hospital and safe. None of all this was any fault of Omri's or anyone's. But he felt terrible—really guilty—about having been so far away.

So it wasn't hard to imagine how badly Little Bear felt the need to get back to help his people. After all, he was their chief; he was responsible for them. Who knew what was happening at the Indian encampment at this very moment? Bright Stars was thinking about it too. She was torn, Omri could see, between wanting to keep Little Bear in bed and wanting him to go back and do what he had to do.

"Let's tell him about Boone's idea," suggested Patrick. "It might take his mind off going back right away himself."

"Yeah! Ah had me a idee, all right!" chimed in Boone. "Say, why don't we all have us a bite t' eat, not to mention a swig o' likker? And talk my idee over? Ain't nuthin' like whiskey fer helpin' yer brain work, ain't that so, kid?"

So Omri crept downstairs and extracted a small glassful of scotch from his parents' drinks cupboard, and some food from the table which his mother had laid for lunch. She was not much of a fancy table-layer, and all there was, for the moment, was Ryvita, butter and some rather tired-looking olives, but that was better than nothing. He grabbed a bit of each and hurried upstairs again.

He should have known better than to leave the room.

As he opened the door, he was greeted by a noise that sounded like a loud chattering of teeth. Then there was a distinct pop, and something went *ping* against the glass of whiskey he was carrying.

His eyes flashed to the cupboard. There, on the shelf in the middle of it, were five miniature soldiers, raking the room with machine-gun fire. On the chest below were several more. They were manning a small but lethal-looking artillery piece.

Omri had no time to think. Dropping everything he threw up his hand to protect his face and dashed forward through a hail of tiny bullets that bit into his palm like wasp stings.

Patrick was standing aghast, too stunned, it seemed, to do anything. Omri fell on the little men in their khaki uniforms, scooped them up, weapons and all, and, shoving them back into the cupboard, slammed the door. He heard another couple of rounds and the muffled boom of an exploding hand grenade against the inside of the door before he could gather his wits and turn the key.

Silence fell in the bedroom.

Omri's first act was to glance over his shoulder to check that Little Bear, Bright Stars and Boone were all right. There was a line of bullet holes through the top of the headboard of the matchbox bed, but mercifully Bright Stars must have persuaded Little Bear to lie down just before the shooting started, and he was okay.

Bright Stars was holding the two horses, which were on Patrick's paddock. They were rearing and plunging with terror, letting out shrill neighs, while Bright Stars hung onto their reins.

Boone was, at first glance, nowhere to be seen, but then Omri made out a tiny pair of cowboy boots and spurs sticking out from under the ramp. He must have dived for cover when the attack began. Not particularly heroic, but certainly by far the most sensible move open to him at the time.

Next, Omri gave his attention to his hand. Half a dozen droplets of blood oozed from as many tiny breaks in the skin. Remembering when Patrick had had a bullet in his cheek from Boone's gun, once, Omri quickly started squeezing out the bullets, lodged just under his skin, between finger and thumbnail. He didn't say a word to Patrick. What was the use? Some people just never learn.

But Patrick had something to say, and in a voice that shook. "I could've got them all killed."

Omri bit his lip. The bullets were actually just visible,

minute black specks. It hurt, getting them out, but it was rather satisfying, like squeezing a blackhead.

"I just wanted to see what would happen," Patrick went on pleadingly.

"Well, now you've seen. Thanks a lot."

"Sorry."

"You're always desperately sorry when you've done something thick."

Patrick didn't argue. He bent down and pulled Boone out from under the ramp by the feet. "It's okay, Boone. They've gone."

The little man was gibbering and shaking from head to foot. "Who in tarnation were those guys?" he managed to ask.

"Soldiers."

"From when?"

"Now. Approximately."

"Boy! Am Ah glad Ah'll be daid before *that* kinda shootin' starts!" he said fervently. "Did they getcha, kid?" he asked Omri anxiously as a drop of blood splashed onto the chest beside him.

"Only a bit," said Omri, pressing a wedge of Kleenex to his hand.

"Did ya git any of the hard stuff?" Boone asked eagerly. "Now Ah *really* need some!"

"Oh—I must've dropped it!"

Boone's face fell. But when Omri went to the door, he found that although the glass had fallen to the floor, spilling most of the scotch, it hadn't broken, and there was still a little left in the bottom. He offered the glass to Boone, who promptly heaved himself up over the rim and dived in head first. Hanging on to the rim by his boots, he started lapping up the dregs of whiskey like a puppy.

Omri couldn't help laughing.

"Oh, come on, Boone! You can't be that thirsty. Remember, you're supposed to be civilized." And he hiked him out and poured the last drops into a toothpaste-cap mug. "Save some for Little Bear."

Boone looked shocked.

"Ya cain't go givin' likker t' Injuns, don't ya know that? Drives 'm crazy. They just ain't got the heads fer it. Anyways, ya couldn't give *him* any. He's too sick."

"When you were wounded you said whiskey made you feel better."

"Yeah, guess Ah did, at that." He gazed sorrowfully down into his mug. "Wal, if'n you're ready t' risk it—only don't blame me if he goes loco—here." He handed the mug to Omri, who passed it to Little Bear, who was sitting up again, examining the bullet holes in his bed.

"Boone sent you some whiskey, Little Bear."

"Not want," said the Indian at once.

"Why not? I thought you liked it."

"Firewater for feast. For make happy. Take from trouble. Little Bear must keep head. Must think, then act. Give firewater Boone. He not need think."

Boone received his drink back without reluctance. Omri picked up some bits of Ryvita and olive from the floor and soon the little people were all munching, though their opinion of olives was evidently not high.

"So mah idee could work," Boone remarked after draining his drink. "Ten fellas like them, with guns like that, an' those Frenchies would be on their knees, if they had any left, beggin' the redskins to make powwow."

Patrick, who had been standing at the window, turned around. "That's what I was thinking," he said.

Omri felt quite exasperated. How could they both be so stupid?

"What do you think, Little Bear?" Patrick asked eagerly. "What if we made lots of soldiers like that real, and then joined them all to you somehow and sent you all back together to your village? They could fight the Frenchmen for you."

Little Bear grew still. His black eyes moved under his scowling brows from one of them to another. For a moment Omri feared he would jump at this tempting solution. But then, reluctantly, he shook his head.

"No good," he said gruffly.

"Aw! Why not? They'd jest shoot'em to mincemeat in

two minutes, and ya'd be rid o' them forever. They'd never dare come back to bother ya no more!"

"Now-soldiers not belong," said Little Bear. "They not fight for Little Bear people. They fight on side of French soldier."

"If at all," said Omri. "Much more likely, they'd just sit down and refuse to fight anyone, once they realized they weren't where they ought to be."

"We could explain to them," said Patrick.

"You try explaining to a whole bunch of soldiers who're probably in the middle of World War II or in Northern Ireland, that they're not to fight the Nazis or the IRA, they're to go off and shoot eighteenth-century Frenchmen in the middle of New York!"

"Well, who *could* you explain it to?"

And that was when Omri had his brain wave.

"I'll tell you who! *Other Indians.*"

Little Bear's head came around. He saw the point at once.

"Yes!" he cried immediately.

"What?" asked Patrick.

"Whatcha mean, kid?" asked Boone.

"Listen, listen!" cried Omri excitedly. "What we have to do is go out and buy loads of Indians. Iroquois, like Little Bear. He'll tell us what sort of clothes and things to look out for—though I think I know anyway. Then we'll bring them to life, and Little Bear can talk to them, and we can send them all back together when Little Bear's better, and—"

"Send back now! Most soon! I well, I better *now*!" Little Bear shouted. Bright Stars came running to calm him, but he wouldn't be calmed. He began shouting at her in their own language. She seemed very excited, and clapped her hands and looked up at Omri with the shining eyes that had given her her name.

"Spirits know Omri save," she said. "Save village, too!"

But Little Bear had something else on his mind. "Now-guns," he said.

"What?" Omri asked, not understanding.

"Now-soldiers no good. But now-guns *good*. Get Iroquois brave, plass-tick, many, many, then give braves now-guns like one make hole in bed."

12

The Troops

THE BOYS ATE LUNCH decorously downstairs, so as not to arouse suspicions, though it was sheer agony to leave the attic bedroom when so much was going on. Little Bear was absolutely in torment, they could see, and though Omri, for his part, was in no hurry to send him back, he felt they must do something as soon as possible to further the plan.

Omri's parents were full of the party they were going to that evening. Adiel and Gillon were going to the movies and were arguing fiercely about which one. Gillon was carrying on a side argument with his parents about the desirability of hiring a video, which, he assured them, would save far more than it cost in the end. Parental reaction to this excellent idea was, as usual, automatic and negative.

All this could not help seeming ridiculously trivial to Omri, with so much on his mind.

They had been out to the model shop before lunch. Omri had taken along one of his books on Indians and tried to find the ones who were dressed in the distinctive Iroquois clothes: floppy leggings with feather decorations, moccasins gathered around the ankles, a sort of sporran-thing hanging like an apron from the waist, turkey feathers in a band around the forehead. Only, there weren't many like that. It was extraordinary what a variety of Indian costumes there were, and the model shop had what appeared to be representatives from a dozen tribes.

Omri knew how bitter the hatred between warring tribes could be. The Algonquins, for instance, were the Iroquois's mortal enemies—it would be no use bringing any of *them*. But since there weren't anything like enough that he was sure were Iroquois, Omri had bought some others he wasn't sure of, in the hope that Little Bear would recognize them as belonging to some friendly Indian nation who would agree to help the Iroquois in their hour of trial.

Patrick, book in hand, was at another shelf, looking at English soldiers of differing periods. He wanted to find some who might have fought the French in America. Omri wasn't keen on bringing any white men into it, but Patrick said they were in it already.

"I bet they'd handle modern weapons better than a bunch of primitive Indians, anyhow."

Omri told him not to be so racist, but when Patrick found some that looked right, according to an illustration in the book, Omri made no objection to buying even one mounted officer. The horse, a handsome black, made him much more expensive.

The whole lot—about fifty assorted Indians and five soldiers—set them back over ten pounds, which for Omri was two weeks' pocket money. Patrick chipped in, though he hadn't brought much.

So now they had this bagful of potential allies for Little Bear and the boys couldn't wait to get started. As soon as lunch was over, the rest of the family scattered and the house became quiet. On the way upstairs, Omri said, "Do you think we dare bring them outdoors?"

"I want to start putting things in the cupboard," said Patrick.

"So do I! I meant, bring the cupboard out too. Then, if any shooting should start, it won't be so dangerous."

"Why should it be less dangerous outdoors?"

"I don't know . . . It just feels as if it would be."

"Well . . . okay. But what if your father or anyone comes out in the garden?"

"Dad's painting in his studio. Anyway there's a hedged-off bit down at the bottom which is just shrubs; he never goes there."

They found the little people waiting for them anxiously.

"Where Omri go so long time?" Little Bear demanded at once.

"Calm down, we've been getting the men."

Little Bear sat up straight, his eyes glowing. "Show!"

"In a minute."

Carefully Omri lifted the matchbox bed onto the seed tray. "Bright Stars, cover him up warmly. We're going outside."

She put the glove-finger around him to the armpits while Boone ran up the ramp and pulled it up behind him. The two ponies were munching grass in their fenced-off paddock. Omri picked the whole thing up, while Patrick took the cupboard and the bag of new men. As an afterthought he slipped Matron in his pocket. Omri did a quick reconnaissance to see that nobody was around. Then they cautiously trooped down the stairs and out the kitchen door into the back garden.

It was really a lovely place, far better than their old garden. It was not just a rectangle of lawn with a few flower beds. It had nooks and crannies. Omri headed for his favorite corner, a clump of bushes with a patch of grass in the middle, where rhododendrons and other tall plants kept prying eyes at bay. The sun was high and the place was sheltered from the wind. Still, Omri suggested Little Bear should be put into the longhouse to keep warm.

"No! Not want! Want be in sun! Sun give *orenda*."

"What's that?"

Little Bear looked baffled. "Not know *orenda*? *Orenda* for all men. Life strength. Sun give. And rain. *Orenda* in animal, plant, all thing. Master of Good make. Now Omri be Master of Good! Make brave, many, fight for Little Bear people."

Omri felt a cold shiver. He didn't like the idea of playing God. But it was too late to back out now.

They laid the seed tray and the cupboard on the grass. Boone at once put the ramp back in position, saddled his pony, tested his lasso, which he kept coiled around the pommel, and set off for a ride. It was rough going, as the grass in the shrubbery was not often mowed, but he didn't seem to mind. "You fellas settle things. Ah'm goin' for a gallop!"

"Keep us in sight," said Patrick.

"That's same as sayin', keep the Rocky Mountains in sight!" laughed Boone. He waved his hat at them and went racing off between the grass-stems shouting "Yippee!" in the approved cowboy fashion. One of the most satisfying things about Boone was the fact that he always behaved exactly as the boys expected. This helped to balance Little Bear. They never knew what to expect from him.

The boys now began to set out the little men they'd bought in lines for Little Bear to inspect. Even though the Indian was well aware they couldn't see him, he seemed to feel ashamed before them, lying in what he called "white man bed." He made Bright Stars help him off it and onto a stack of rhododendron leaves he ordered to be laid on the earth. It looked very grand, like stiff layers of shiny dark green leather, but not very comfortable, Omri thought.

Little Bear sat cross-legged and stared narrowly at the Indian figures one by one. Several times he demanded that one of them be brought and laid before him for closer inspection. Some he discarded with an imperious wave of his hand. Once, he uttered a deep growl.

"Why bring Algonquin enemy?"

"Sorry," said Omri, hastily removing the offending figure. "I thought he was a Mohawk. He dresses like one."

"Mohawk part of *Iroquois* nation. Omri not see difference? Stupid. Big eyes not best."

About three quarters of the men they'd bought were eventually approved. Then Little Bear turned his eyes to the British soldiers.

They were rather splendid in their white breeches, scarlet coats, and three-cornered hats, but Omri didn't think they looked very businesslike. The white bands crossed on their chests and backs made ideal targets. But perhaps the brilliance of their uniforms was intended to intimidate the enemy. Anyway they were all armed with muskets tipped with fearsome-looking blades. Omri bent one easily with his finger, thinking how sharp and lethal they would be when the cupboard had done its work and these bayonet swords became gleaming steel.

"These no good," Little Bear pronounced abruptly.

Patrick and Omri were astonished.

"What's wrong with them?" said Patrick. "Are they from the wrong time?"

"Right time. Near right. English soldier like that fight French in big battle soon before. French win."

"Oh! Why?"

"Fight better. But also English dress stupid. This—this—" He pointed contemptuously to the red coats and white trimmings. "Catch sun. Call eye of French soldier. Gun point. Pshooo!" He made a shooting noise. "No good if soldier proud. Must dress so enemy not see."

"How do the English soldiers dress—er—now?"

"More like Indian. Earth colors. Like leaf. Shadow. More good for hide. Jump out on enemy. White man learn much from Indian."

"Now who's proud?" Patrick whispered to Omri.

"LITTLE BEAR HEAR THAT!" the Indian roared. Really, he had ears like a bat.

"Well, anyway, so you don't want us to bring these men

to life?" said Patrick hurriedly.

"Not need. Enough with braves and now-guns."

The boys exchanged glances. This was tricky. Little Bear *was* proud and he wouldn't like the suggestion that the white men might be better with modern weapons.

"Listen, Little Bear—" Omri began coaxingly.

Suddenly they froze. Omri heard his mother's voice calling him from the house.

"Omri! *Omri!*"

"What?" he called back, getting quickly to his feet.

"Darling, Kitsa's caught a bird! Or a mouse or something. Anyway, she's playing with it on the big lawn. Can you—?"

Omri's mind seemed to blow hollow like an egg. He stopped hearing what his mother was saying. But Patrick was up and off in a flash, charging through the bushes like a madman. Omri came behind him, the branches smacking him across the face.

On the main lawn was Kitsa, her blackness and whiteness beautiful, sleek and deadly in the sunshine. She was crouched and concentrated; her tail tip just twitching, all else about her perfectly still.

There was something small and helpless and alive in the grass in front of her.

13

A Death and a Healing

"**K**ITSA!"

Omri screamed out her name. Startled, she turned her head. Both boys were pelting towards her. Furious at the interruption, she turned back and with one quick wiggle of her hips, she pounced. At almost the same second, Patrick reached her.

Without time to think, he kicked her, or rather, kicked at her. She started to jump away at the same second so that his foot, though it did just about connect with her, merely accelerated her flight through the air. With a yowl of outrage, empty-mouthed and thwarted, she fled.

Omri and Patrick fell to their knees on the spot Kitsa had so hastily vacated.

The white horse was lying on its side. Its legs were moving but it was obviously hurt. It kept raising its head and whinnying and then letting its head drop back again. Boone was lying half under it. He didn't move.

Patrick very gently shifted the pony until he could lift Boone clear. Suddenly Boone shot to his feet and shouted, "Am Ah daid? Did it kill me?"

"You look okay to me," said Patrick. His voice sounded to Omri like the voice of a complete stranger. It was deep and gruff, like a man's. Boone was looking around in a daze.

"Whut was it?"

"A cat."

"A *cat*! It was the biggest danged critter Ah ever seen in mah en-tire life! It jest come from nowhere—one minute Ah was ridin' along, mindin' mah own business, and sud-denly—"

Then his eyes fell on his horse.

It raised its head again and whickered softly, as if asking him to help it. There was a terrible moment of silence. Boone crouched by the horse's head, stroking it, running his hands over it. He unbuckled the saddle and lifted it clear, and very gently ran his hands over its white side.

Then he took off his hat. It was a strange gesture. Omri had seen men do it in films when they heard of someone's death. A gesture of respect, of something stronger than respect. Boone stood up.

"Ribs is broke," he said. "Have t' finish him."

"*Oh, no*!" Omri heard himself say in a desperate voice.

"Ain't no use keepin' him alive t' suffer. He's mah pal."

His voice, which cracked and dissolved into tears at the least thing, was now perfectly steady.

Slowly he reached for his revolver.

Omri couldn't bear it. "Please, Boone! Don't! Surely we can save him!"

Boone shook his head. "He's too far gone. I gotta do it." He looked up again. His face was strained but dry-eyed. "You boys turn yer backs. This ain't fer kids to see."

Omri turned his back. Patrick didn't. Boone bent down. He whispered something briefly into the horse's ear. Then he put his revolver to its head. Omri didn't see this, but he heard the shot. Tears spurted from his eyes. He couldn't check them. He wiped them hard and furiously with both hands.

Why should he, who hardly ever cried anymore, cry over the death of Boone's horse, when Boone, who cried all the time, was so controlled? Turning around, seeing Boone standing quietly beside the horse's body with his hat in one hand and his smoking revolver in the other, Omri tried to feel ashamed of his own weakness, but he couldn't. It was his fault, partly, that this disaster had happened. They had been so preoccupied with the Plan and the exciting prospect of bringing more little people to life that they had let Boone ride off into a monstrous wilderness, full of deadly dangers. That it should have been Omri's own beloved little cat who had done this, just made everything worse.

Irrational fury seized him. He crouched down. "I'll kill her," he ground out between his teeth.

Boone looked up at him.

"Don't you kill nuthin', kid. Th' critter wuz only follerin' its instincks. Ya cain't blame a cat fer *bein'* a cat, even if'n it do fall on a fella as fierce and sudden as a Texas hurricane."

"I'll—we'll get you another horse."

"Yeah, you do that. Ah'll git to be pals with it, same as I wuz with this'n. Someday. Ah guess. A man ain't whole without a hoss."

He replaced his gun in its holster. "Jest now kin Ah have a shovel?"

Patrick swallowed, cleared his throat and said, "We'll bury him for you, Boone."

"Thanks, son, Ah'd be obliged t' ya."

Omri fetched a trowel from the greenhouse and dug a small hole in a flower bed just under a nodding chrysanthemum. Boone took the bridle off the horse and laid the saddle over his arm. Then Patrick picked up the body. It was still warm, and strangely heavy for its size. He laid it in the hole and Omri covered it up and made a little mound. They stood for a moment. Then Boone settled his hat back on his ginger head.

"C'mon, then," he said. "We'd best be gittin' back t' th' others, before somethin' happens to *them.*"

Patrick carried the cowboy back through the rhododendrons.

There was no sign of Little Bear and Bright Stars, and for a moment Omri's heart seemed to leap into his mouth. But then Little Bear walked—actually walked, though slowly and unsteadily—out of the ruined longhouse.

"Where you go? Why leave?" he demanded.

Patrick stooped and opened his hand so Boone could step out onto the seed tray. As far as Omri could judge, the cowboy looked as always; but Little Bear seemed to know at once that something had happened. He even guessed what.

"Where horse?" he asked Boone.

"Daid," Boone answered shortly.

No more was said, but the Indian touched Boone briefly on the shoulder before turning back to Omri.

"Now we put braves in box."

But this time it was Patrick who had been doing some thinking.

"Just a minute, Little Bear."

Little Bear turned to him. "What minute? Do now!"

"Okay, so say we bring forty Indians to life. Then what?—I mean, what will happen right away? Because you can't go back and start fighting the French right away."

"I go back ry-taway! Why no?"

"Because you're not well enough. No, Little Bear! You can't be. So we'll have forty other people on our hands. We'll have to feed them and look after them until you're ready. That might be days—weeks."

"Who weak? I strong!"

"Seven days," said Patrick, holding up seven fingers. "That's a week."

Little Bear glowered. "No week. No wait. If stay here, not help tribe, they make new chief."

"I tell you what," said Patrick. He reached into his pocket. "We'll get Matron back. See what she says."

"May Tron?"

"Yes." Patrick held up the formidable little figure in her tall cap.

Little Bear made a face. "What use white woman with face like old beaver?"

"She saved your life, so you'd better not be rude. She's like a doctor."

Little Bear looked shocked. "No woman, doctor!" he exclaimed.

"Well, this one is. She took the metal out of your back last night. If she says you're healed enough to fight, okay, we'll get started on your army. If not—we'll wait."

And he put Matron in the cupboard.

When he opened the door, she was standing blinking at the sudden sunlight. She had a newly starched cap perched on her head.

"Ah-ha!" she cried when she saw the boys. "I thought as much! The more I thought about it, the more certain I was you'd need me again! So, do you know what I did? I popped a few things into my apron pocket, just in case."

She hitched up her skirt and climbed over the rim of the cupboard.

"Think ahead," she said. "That's my motto." Then she saw Little Bear standing before her with folded arms and uttered a shriek, but it was not of terror.

"What on *earth* are you doing out of bed! Are you trying to kill yourself?"

"Not kill self," said Little Bear calmly. "Maybe kill you."

She bore down upon him. "Nonsense, my good man, you're delirious, and no wonder. This is absolutely outrageous, twenty-four hours after—ahem!—*major* surgery and here you are, on your feet instead of flat on your back—I mean, on your front! Lie down *at once*!"

To the amazement of the boys, and no less perhaps to Little Bear's own surprise, he found himself obeying her commands. Clearly it never occurred to her that he wouldn't. He lay down on the pile of leaves and she knelt to examine

111

him. Bright Stars ran to help her. Together they took off the dressings. Matron peered closely at the wounds, then sat back on her heels.

"Unbelievable," she said. "Fantastic! If I didn't see it I would never credit it. Beautiful! You know," she went on as she took a tiny bottle and some cotton from her capacious pocket, "the trouble is, *we* live an entirely unnatural and unhealthful life. Eat the wrong foods, don't exercise enough . . . Look at this man. Just look! Superb specimen. Not an ounce of fat on him. Bright eyes, perfect teeth, skin and hair gleaming with health—splendid! And if something does go wrong, his magnificent, well-oiled defense

system springs into action and hey presto! He's practically healed."

She washed the wounds, then took out a hypodermic needle, and squirted it briefly at the sky.

"Just to be on the safe side," she said. "Trousers down!" And before Little Bear could grasp her intention, she had pulled his buckskins down and plunged the needle into his bottom.

Little Bear had borne a lot of pain without a flinch, but this humiliation was too much. He let out a roar as if he'd been gored by a buffalo.

"*What* a silly fuss! There! All over!" said Matron brightly, withdrawing the needle and rubbing the spot briskly with the cotton. "Just in case of infection, but really there's little fear of that. He's practically as good as new. What a constitution! Of course," she added modestly, "I didn't do a bad job on him, if I do say so myself."

"Would you think he'd be well enough to—well, to do something—pretty active?" Omri asked.

"Try stopping him," said Matron. She rose to her feet and dusted the earth off her knees. "Personally, if he were on *my* ward I'd say bed rest for another day or so, but a body like his knows its own business best."

"Could he ride, say?"

"That's up to the horse!" quipped Matron, laughing rather horsily herself. "Well, I must be off!"

Meanwhile, Little Bear, who had scrambled hastily to his feet, now drew his knife and threatened her with it. But Matron, not at all alarmed, wagged her finger at him.

"Tsk, tsk, naughty man! That would never do at St. Thomas's." She turned her back on him without a qualm. Baffled, he lowered the knife. "Astonishing, these primitives," she remarked to Omri as she strode back to the cupboard. "Perfect control over the body—none at all over the emotions."

Back in the cupboard she offered Omri her hand, and then burst out laughing again.

"Aren't I silly? How could we shake hands? Oh, but do try! I'd just love to shake hands with a giant, even if it is all a very convincing dream." Omri took her tiny hand between finger and thumb and solemnly shook it.

"Cheerio! Do call on me in any future hour of need!"

"We will," said Omri, closing the door.

He turned from the cabinet to find Little Bear's eyes fixed on him.

"Old white she-bear say I good," he said. "Now Patrick, Omri, keep word."

The boys looked at each other.

"Right," said Omri, taking a deep breath. "Let's get started."

14

Red Men, Red Coats

BRINGING FORTY INDIANS to life sounds like quite an undertaking, but it took a remarkably short time to accomplish. They did a few first, just to be on the safe side; but when the first half dozen had clambered out of the cupboard and were at once greeted by Little Bear, who regaled them in his strange language, which they all seemed to understand, Omri and Patrick didn't delay further.

"Let's put all the rest in at once!" said Patrick excitedly, and this time Omri made no objections.

Soon the seed tray was jammed with men, milling around, sitting on Patrick's fence, admiring Little Bear's pony, exclaiming in dismay at the ruined longhouse, gazing covertly at Bright Stars and examining the paintings on the side of the tepee. One or two tried to enter this, but Little Bear barred the way. Boone was in there. None of them knew how the Indians might react to him, so they'd decided to hide him.

The new Indians didn't pay any attention to the boys at first, or to anything in what, to them, was the distance. Everything on the seed tray was in scale with them, and soon they settled down in rows, cross-legged, to listen to what Little Bear had to say.

He dragged the matchbox bed into position before the tepee and stood on it, making it a platform. From there he addressed them in a loud, commanding tone for several minutes.

Omri and Patrick sat well back, shaded by bushes.

"It was a good idea of yours to be outdoors," whispered Patrick. "Seems more natural, and there aren't huge bits of furniture and so on to worry them."

Omri didn't react to this praise for his idea. If they had stayed inside, Boone's horse would still be alive.

They watched. After a while, Little Bear stopped speaking and beckoned imperiously to the boys, who crawled forward on their knees till they hung over the seed tray. Little Bear pointed to them dramatically, and all the little Indians turned to look.

Their reaction was curiously unsensational. Some uttered muted cries; one or two leapt to their feet, but then sank down again after glancing at Little Bear and seeing him unafraid. Evidently he had given them some explanation for the presence of giants in their midst, which they had no difficulty in accepting. The "Great Spirits" business, no doubt. Omri couldn't help smiling at Little Bear's obvious pride in having such beings at his command. It clearly gave him a lot of prestige in the eyes of these tribesmen he was hoping to lead into battle.

After a few more words to his audience, Little Bear turned to the boys.

"Make now-guns," he ordered.

They knelt, irresolute. Omri had never really taken to the idea of Indians running amok with machine guns, hand grenades and artillery. Anything could happen, especially if they got overexcited. But Little Bear was scowling horribly at their hesitation.

"Make now-guns *now*!" he thundered. "Little Bear give word to braves!"

"Oh, dear," said Patrick ironically. "That does it, then. I'd better fetch them."

He jumped to his feet. Omri said, "While you're in the house, ask my mum to give you something for us to eat. For *them* to eat."

"Anything else you can think of?"

"Yes. Bring some horses for Boone to choose from."

"One thing at a time," said Patrick. "Boone'd better stay

out of sight." And he pushed off through the bushes.

While he was gone, Omri thought he ought to have a word with Little Bear.

"These now-guns, as you call them, are very, very powerful. And they're complicated. They can't be used without special training."

Little Bear curled his lip in scorn.

"I see what soldier do. Point gun. Pull trigger, like gun French, English soldier fight with Indian. But kill more! Shoot many, many!" Little Bear made a noise like the chatter of a machine gun. The other Indians reacted with excitement.

"But the bigger ones—"

"Omri show how!"

"You don't think *I* know, do you? As you keep reminding me, I'm only a boy."

Little Bear frowned. The rows of seated Indians below him seemed to sense his doubt, and began murmuring to each other uneasily. Little Bear raised his hand to silence them.

"Omri put now-soldier in box. Him show."

Omri considered. There was actually no option to bringing some modern soldiers to life, however briefly, because their plastic figures were attached to their weapons. Omri's plan had been to do as he had done once before, when he'd wanted a bow and arrows for Little Bear.

He had brought an old Indian to life and taken his weapons from him, meaning to transform him at once back into plastic. But he had promptly dropped dead of a heart attack. Omri thought that some artillery sergeant might be made of sterner stuff. Perhaps it would be worth a try.

"And what about these?" he asked, holding up a soldier from the time of George the Third (who, according to a verse Omri recalled from somewhere, "ought never to have occurred").

"Try," said Little Bear tersely.

Feeling a bit guilty at doing it without Patrick, Omri put the five scarlet-clad soldiers into the cupboard. At once the clattering of metal on metal announced that the soldiers and their mounted officer were ready to emerge.

"Little Bear, you'd better go in there with them. Better if you talk to them first, and decide if you want them."

"Good!"

Omri opened the door a crack and Little Bear slipped over the edge of the seed tray straight into the cupboard. Omri put his ear to the opening at the top to listen.

Little Bear began at once to harangue the British officer in his broken English. Omri heard the word "French" and the word "kill" but he couldn't make out much more until the shrill bark of an English voice cut him short.

"Who do you think you are, giving orders to an officer of His Majesty's 20th American Regiment, you filthy savage!"

There was a deathly silence. Then Little Bear shouted: "I no savage! I Iroquois chief! Iroquois fight at side of English soldier! English happy have Indian help, braves spill blood in English quarrel, now I ask help from English! Why redcoat give insult?"

There was a brief pause, and then the English voice said, with icy contempt: "Insolent bounder! Kill him, Smithers."

Omri put his hand on the door to slam it shut, but another voice spoke.

"Is that wise, sir? After all, we have used them in the past."

"Plenty more where he came from."

"But if he's a chief, sir—might lead to trouble—"

"Of course, Smithers, if you're squeamish, I'll do it myself!—Here! Come back, you blackguard—"

But it was too late. Little Bear had already slipped silently over the bottom rim of the cupboard and was throwing his weight against the door. Omri was very happy to assist him, and in short order the arrogant British redcoats were reduced to their plastic condition again.

Little Bear, his eyes slits of rage and every tooth in his head bared, gave Omri a look of reproach. Omri felt he was being blamed just because he was English too.

"Surely they're not all like that," he muttered.

"Some English no better than French" was all Little

Bear had to say. "Braves fight alone."

Just then, Patrick came crashing back through the rhododendrons. He had a tray in his hand, on which were two glasses of milk, two packets of salted peanuts and a couple of red apples. Also a paper bag containing the "now-soldiers." Omri only hoped they might do something to redeem the character of the British Army in the eyes of his Indian.

There was a pleasant interlude while they fed the Indians. They crushed some of the nuts between two more or less clean stones and served the bits on platters made from the round leaves of a nasturtium. Patrick bit a piece off one of the apples and broke it up small, while Omri filled and refilled the toothpaste caps which were passed reverently from hand to hand along the rows of seated braves. Among them, they put away nearly half a glass of milk.

Boone, who had been peeping from behind the flap of the tepee, sent a private message with Bright Stars, suggesting a bit of "the hard stuff" should be added to the milk "to put fire in belly," as Bright Stars solemnly explained. Boone evidently felt it would be no bad thing if these Indians did go a bit loco. But Omri and Patrick agreed that everyone ought to keep a clear head.

Then it was time to bring the modern soldiers to life again and see what could be done about guns.

After consultation with Little Bear, they began with a hulking Royal Marine corporal, kneeling behind his machine gun. He was the one who had sprayed Omri with bullets, so Omri had a sort of warped affection for him.

"We can't risk Little Bear again," said Omri. He had told Patrick what had happened with the eighteenth-century soldiers. "A modern soldier would probably be just as unbelieving about a Red Indian as he would about finding himself tiny."

"We'll just have to hope he can accept it, somehow. After all, he's seen us once, the first shock's over. Come on, no good putting it off."

Patrick slipped the corporal into the cupboard.

15

Corporal Fickits

"WE'LL HAVE TO WATCH IT. Last time I did this, they all just started shooting like mad the second the door opened."

So they opened the door the merest crack at first, and Omri put his mouth to it and said, "Don't shoot! We want to talk to you."

A very ripe soldierly oath answered him, followed by: ". . . I've gorn off me trolley again!"

"Just don't shoot. Okay?" And Omri slowly swung the cupboard door open.

The corporal had stood up. He gazed around. The machine gun gleamed in the sun, oiled and ready for action.

"Blimey, now I'm outdoors! What the 'ell is goin' on?"

Omri went into his spiel. "Of course it must seem incredible, but the fact is, for the moment you've become small. You can tell your grandchildren about it . . . And it's going to get even more interesting. What we want is for you to tell some friends of ours, who are your size, how to work your machine gun."

"And 'oo are they planning to shoot wiv it, if it's not a rude answer?"

"Well, you see—" But it was too complicated. Omri looked helplessly at Patrick.

"Who do you shoot with it?" Patrick cut in quickly.

The man gave a barking laugh. "The Queen's enemies, and anyone else who looks sideways at the Royal Marines."

"And are you an expert on guns—I mean all kinds?"

"You could say so. We're trained to 'andle just about anything. *And* anybody."

The boys gave each other a quick look. This suited them.

"Right," said Patrick briskly. "Here's your chance to prove it. I'm going to put you and your machine gun in front of a bunch of men. And you're going to demonstrate how to use it. You'll go through it once, and then let some of them try it. Only, be careful, we don't want anybody hurt—this is only a training exercise."

The corporal's face had gone rigid and he stood at attention while Patrick spoke. Then he gave a smart salute.

"Sir!"

"What's your name, Corporal?"

"Fickits, sir, Corporal Royal Marines Willy Fickits."

"How much ammunition have you, Corporal?"

"Three 'undred rounds, sir."

"Don't waste any."

"Sir!"

"Now, don't be scared when I pick you up."

The corporal's adam's apple jumped as he swallowed, but his face didn't change.

"Sir!"

Patrick carried the man, stiff as a tiny pencil, between finger and thumb and set him down, still at attention, on the platform. At the sight of him there was a buzz of astonished interest among the Indians, most of whom leapt to their feet. The corporal allowed his eyes to rove briefly across the mass of half-naked redskins. His adam's apple did a jig in his throat and his eyes popped. Then his rigid expression came back.

Meanwhile Omri had carefully lifted the machine gun out of the cupboard and set it beside him. The nearness of his weapon seemed to restore him.

"Begin, Corporal!" said Patrick, who found he rather liked giving orders he knew would be instantly obeyed.

"Right, men!" Fickits barked. "Pay attention! I am about to demonstrate the workings of this 'ere weapon, a marvel of military science. I will first break it dahn and put it back together—"

"Never mind that, Fickits," interrupted Patrick. "Just show them how to shoot with it."

The corporal instantly changed tack.

"I will first demonstrate the method of firing." He dropped to one knee, aimed over the heads of the crowd, and fired off a short but noisy burst. Bullets whistled through the air and caused a flurry among the rhododendron leaves.

The Indians watched this impassively. They didn't seem to grasp what had happened. But Little Bear leapt up beside Fickits and shouted something. He must have told them that each bang represented a bullet, or with luck a dead enemy. At that, the Indians jumped up and started yelling excitedly and pushing towards the platform. Almost at once a fight broke out among those wanting to be the first to try the gun. Corporal Fickits stared at the scrimmage in dismay.

"You'd better give these blighters some orders, sir!" he shouted at Patrick above the uproar. "Goin' on like that, it won't do, sir!"

"It's your gun, Corporal! *You* give the orders!"

"*Me*, sir? Ain't there an officer about, sir? Or at least a sergeant!"

The scrimmage below was getting wilder. One burly Indian had already laid two others out cold and was scrambling up onto the platform.

"You're in charge, Corporal! Go on, tell them to behave. They'll listen to you!"

After a baffled moment, Fickits saw that the Indian had laid hands on his gun and was swinging the barrel wildly in all directions. This galvanised him into action.

"TAKE YER 'ANDS ORF THAT GUN!" he bellowed.

His voice was not that of a corporal, but of a regimental sergeant major. All at once the howling mob of Indians fell silent. Even Little Bear looked impressed. The Indian at the gun found himself hiked upright by his hair (all Fickits had to get hold of) and flung off the platform.

"Nah then, you bunch of 'orrible little men!" roared Fickits. "You touch this 'ere weapon when *I* says you will touch it, and NOT BEFOWER, DO YOU UNDERSTAND THAT? Or you will find yourselves wishin' that your mothers 'ad never met your fathers, IS THAT CLEAR???"

There was a profound silence. Even the birds in the bushes seemed stunned.

"Wow," breathed Patrick. "That's telling them."

Corporal Fickits proved a godsend. He knew a great deal about military hardware, not only machine guns. As fast as Omri put the soldiers into the cupboard, made their weapons real, removed them from their owners, and placed them on the matchbox platform, Fickits instructed his now-obedient students how to work them. Soon they had two field guns, ten hand grenades, three bazookas, two more machine guns, and a small pile of automatic rifles. The Indians appeared to like these best. When they discovered that they could actually run while firing them, it took all Corporal Fickits's newfound authority to keep any kind of order, and even so it was a miracle that no one got hurt during the training. The boys set up stripped twigs and round pieces of trimmed bark as targets, but as there was a limited amount of ammunition, every Indian was given only five rounds to practice with.

Fickits was uneasy about the larger guns.

"Firing artillery, sir, ain't something you do any old

how. Any 'alfwit can blast off with the 'andguns, sir, or throw a grenade, but if you'll take my advice you'll leave the ordnance pieces out of it. You need a properly trained crew for artillery, sir. Not rabble like this lot, sir."

"If that's your advice, Corporal, we'll follow it," said Patrick.

Corporal Fickits's expression did not change, but he seemed to swell up inside his uniform like a miniature pouter pigeon.

"Thankysir!" he said, making it all one word.

Little Bear was getting impatient.

"Braves know shoot now-guns," he said urgently. "Time go back!"

Omri had been, he now realized, secretly dreading this moment. There was his Indian, not yet fully recovered, no matter what anyone said, about to be plunged into a life-or-death situation.

But he knew there was no way to avoid it. People had to do what they had to do. However, that didn't mean Bright Stars had to go into danger.

"Can you leave Bright Stars here?" Omri asked.

"Yes," said Little Bear. "Leave wife. Omri take care. Bring old white she-bear when time come for Little Bear son. But no let stab with claw in backside!"

Omri and the Indian looked at each other for a moment.

"Good luck," said Omri.

"Need help from Great Spirits. Then fight well, win against French, Algonquin enemy."

"Did the Algonquins help attack your village?"

"Algonquin lead. French follow. Now go back. Take vengeance."

"I wish I could see it," said Omri.

"And me," added Patrick, who had overheard.

It took some time to assemble the now heavily armed Indian troop and prepare them to leave. Bright Stars directed Omri to bring her some flowers, which she crushed in her hands, producing a colored pulp with which she smeared Little Bear's face in streaks. Others were decorating themselves with mixtures of mud and some other colors they had had with them.

Every time a bird flew overhead they all looked up apprehensively. Omri thought they were afraid it might attack them (as indeed it might, had the boys not been there to guard them) but Little Bear, after one such overpass, said:

"Bad omen if shadow fall on braves before battle."

The last Indians were leaving Bright Stars's pool, smearing patterns of mud on their torsos. Omri looked at the now murky water in the coffee-jar lid. It had a reddish look where the sinking sun caught it. He turned away, glad that *he* didn't believe in omens.

16

"If'n Ya Wanna Go Back . . ."

ORPORAL FICKITS MARCHED his troops into the cupboard and lined them up in two ranks in the bottom of it. The machine guns were lifted in. Fickits saluted Patrick. "Trainees drawn up and ready, sir!"

"Thanks, Corporal. You've done a good job."

"Thankysir."

"Now you're going back where you came from, Fickits. Don't forget how it feels to give orders. You'll be a sergeant in no time."

Fickits permitted himself a grin. "Yessir. Thankysir."

Omri told Little Bear to instruct his men each to put a hand on the shoulder of the man beside or in front of him, so the whole group was physically linked. "And they must all be linked to you, Little Bear, so you'll take them back with you."

Little Bear was in the paddock, fetching his pony. He had to get Bright Stars to give him a leg up. He bent over and put his hand on her black head. She gazed up at him, her eyes sparkling, this time with tears. She seemed to be begging him for something, but he shook his head. Suddenly she reached up, seized his hand, and pressed it to her cheek. Then she turned and ran into the tepee.

As she entered, Boone's face appeared at the flap.

"Hey! Pssst! Injun!"

Little Bear, who was riding toward the ramp, turned his head.

"Give it to those Frenchies!"

"I give."

Little Bear mounted, waved at the boys, rode down the ramp and, catching the reins up chest-high, galloped to the cupboard. His pony jumped the bottom rim and swerved to a sudden stop to avoid the ranks of Indians. Little Bear barked a command. All the Indians put their hands on each other's shoulders. The nearest brave put his on the pony's rump.

"Omri shut door, send!" ordered Little Bear. His face was burning with impatience.

Omri gave himself a second to take in the group. The

painted braves in their double row looked proud, ferocious, eager. They were obviously looking forward to the
coming battle without a trace of fear. The weaponry caught
the sun and glistened with readiness to do what it had been
made to do. For a moment, Omri was swamped by doubts.
It was like . . . like *mailing death*. Why should he help to
kill people . . . ? But he was caught up in it now.

"Go on!" urged Patrick. "Send them!"

"Wait—Fickits!" said Omri. He picked up the little
corporal, who was standing at attention just outside the
cupboard, and set him by himself on the shelf. Then he
shut the door firmly and turned the key.

For a long moment, they didn't breathe. Then Omri
opened the door. His hand was shaking and he jiggled the
cupboard a bit as he did it. Two or three of the Indian figures, now plastic, fell over. It was like dominoes, each
knocking down another until most of them lay tumbled
across each other on the floor of the cupboard. Only Little
Bear and Fickits and a couple more were still upright.

The boys stared at the scene in a dismay they couldn't
control. Boone, who had crept to the edge of the seed tray
and was leaning over to look, voiced their feeling.

"Looks like a massacree, don't it?"

"Don't be stupid, Boone!" Patrick almost shouted.
"They're just plastic now. They fell over because Omri

jogged the cupboard."

"Sure," said Boone hastily. "Sure, Ah know that! Ah wuz just sayin'—"

"Well, don't!"

"You ain't superstitious, are ya?"

"Of course not!"

Now there was a feeling of intense anticlimax. There seemed nothing they ought to do. It was getting chilly. They sat for a bit, but that became intolerable because of what they were all imagining.

"Let's go in."

Again Patrick took the cupboard, with its contents, and the bag of weaponless British soldiers, and Omri took the seed tray.

Bright Stars and Boone retreated into the tepee, just in case they met anyone on the way back upstairs, which was just as well, because as they passed Gillon's bedroom on the first floor, the door opened and out he came.

Omri and Patrick started guiltily. They couldn't help it.

"What's all that?" Gillon asked, not because he particularly wanted to know but just out of idle curiosity.

"Just some stuff we've been mucking about with," said Omri. He tried to push past, but Gillon stood in his path.

"Oh, it's that fantastic little house you made last year," said Gillon. "And the leather tepee. Often wondered what had happened to that. Never seen one like it in the shops. . ." Before they could do anything, he'd picked the tepee up to examine it.

It was one of the worst moments of Omri's life. There was nothing he could do. There were Bright Stars and Boone, crouching on the earth, exposed—discovered. Everything seemed frozen—neither Patrick nor Omri could move, and the little people sat absolutely motionless. Omri's eyes were fastened to them helplessly. They were so obviously alive—so vulnerable! He waited, as a condemned man waits for the ax to fall on his neck, for Gillon to notice them.

Gillon, however, was looking only at the tepee in his hands.

"This really is a mini-marvel," he said. "I love the paintings. Has Dad seen these?" He peered closer. "This little beaver—and the porcupine . . . they look dead *genuine*, like those cave paintings we saw in France . . . And the way the poles are attached, inside, it's really a work of art."

With that he plonked it carelessly back on the earth, nearly knocking Boone's head off, and swung away down the stairs singing a pop song at the top of his lungs.

Patrick did a perfect imitation of Matron, spinning on his heel and falling in a mock faint on the landing. He lay there with the cupboard on his stomach and his eyes wide open and crossed. After a second he sat up.

"Whew, that was close!"

Omri was still rooted to the spot. Boone was lying, half in, half out of the tepee, on his back. His eyes looked crossed too—quite genuinely. After a few moments he wriggled all the way out and stood up, wiping the sweat off his face.

"Jeez, son," he complained, "d' ya have t' skeer a fella like that? *An*' the li'l lady . . . 'Tain't right, with her bein' the way she is, skeerin' her that-a-way. Might bring somethin' on."

Omri put his face down and whispered through the flap. "Are you okay, Bright Stars?"

There was no answer. Cautiously Omri lifted the tepee again. Bright Stars was sitting perfectly still, her face down on her knees.

"Bright Stars? Answer me!"

Patrick had stood up and was peering anxiously over Omri's shoulder.

"What's wrong?"

"I don't know. Let's get up to my room."

They went up. Omri carried the seed tray very carefully. Inside, they locked the door and put the seed tray and the cupboard down on Omri's desk and turned on the lamp.

Bright Stars stood up. Her face had a greyish look under the brown.

"Son come now," she said clearly.

"Ah knew it!" said Boone. "Git that ol' bat in the white headpiece back."

"Bright Stars need no one. Need water. Knife. Omri bring, then leave." She signed that he should put the tepee back to cover her.

"Are you sure, Bright Stars? Little Bear said—"

"Little Bear go fight. Bright Stars make son. Go."

Though very uneasy, Omri obeyed her. He fetched some boiled water, cleaned out the pond and refilled it. Boone carried a bucketful of water to the flap of the tepee and laid his pocketknife beside it. "That's t' cut the cord, y' know," he confided. "Animals bite it through, but Ah guess th' Injuns is beyond that."

After a short time, Bright Stars's hand came out through the flap of the tepee and took in the bucket and then the knife. After that, she fastened the flap firmly shut, and all was quiet.

There seemed nothing to do but wait. Omri knew that with white people, anyway, the first baby often took a long time to be born. His mother had been half a day producing Adiel, she'd told them. Perhaps with Indians it was different.

Patrick was uneasy. "If anything happened to her, Little Bear wouldn't ever forgive us! I wish he'd taken her back with him. Shouldn't we bring Matron?"

"Bright Stars said not to. Matron's awfully bossy. Maybe she'd just upset her."

137

"Well, I think she'd be better off back in her own village."

"I *wish* I knew what was happening—back there!" Omri burst out.

"Yeah! If only *we* could get back somehow."

They sat, the three of them, the boys on chairs, Boone on the "couch" of rhododendron leaves where Little Bear had sat. Every now and then, Boone stood up and paced the ground outside the tepee. He kept biting hunks off a block of tobacco he had with him and chewing at it and then spitting it out. He was obviously very worked up.

Finally he stopped.

"Ah shoulda gone with 'em," he said. "Ah knew at the time Ah shoulda."

"That would've been crazy, Boone," said Patrick. "Someone would have shot you just because you look different, and you're white."

"Mebbe Ah could've stayed in the tepee and shot the Frenchies from cover. Ah could've done *somethin'*. Thet Injun's mah blood brother. His fight oughta be mah fight!"

"We need you here, Boone."

"Whut fur? Ah ain't no use here!"

"Well," said Omri, "you can help with the baby."

Boone's jaw dropped. "*Me?* Watcha take me for? Babies is wimmin's bizness!"

Just at that moment, they heard a little cry from inside

the tepee. It wasn't a baby's cry. In a flash Boone was crouched at the flap.

"Lemme in, lady, ya cain't be alone in thur! Ah'll help ya! Ah brung a dozen calves into the world, *an'* a foal once't, an' they're a lot bigger'n a baby—Ah know whut t'do!"

There was a pause, and then a slight movement at the tent flap. Boone grinned a rather wobbly grin over his shoulder at the boys.

"Ya see? She trusts me," he said. "Don't fret, now. Li'l Bear'll be glad he made me his brother, you wait." The flap was loosened and Boone started to crawl in. But just before he disappeared, he turned once more.

"Ah wuz thinkin'," he said. "If'n ya really wanted to go back, and watch the battle—"

The boys looked at each other, then leaned forward incredulously to listen.

"Wal, whut Ah wuz wonderin' wuz . . . Does it have t'be the cupboard? Mebbe it ain't the cupboard so much as that thur fancy key. Did ya ever try the key in somethin' bigger? Like that great big box, for instance, that we wuz all on before."

Another little cry, more of a gasp, came from inside the tepee.

"S' long, boys—wish us luck!" Boone said, and crawled the rest of the way, leaving both boys in a ferment of excitement at the possibilities of this amazing new idea.

17

As Far As You Can Go

"**W**OULD IT WORK?"

"How do I know? I never thought of it."

"We never asked ourselves whether the cupboard was part of what makes it happen. Maybe he's right. Maybe the cupboard's just a cupboard, and the magic thing is the key."

They turned both at once to look at the chest.

The top of it still had scattered bits of Kleenex, boxes and other things on it. Omri went over to it and swept all this off. Then he opened it. It was full of his private stuff.

"It's not big enough to hold both of us at once."

"We couldn't both go together anyway, you wally."

"Why not?" Then he realized. Of course! Someone would have to stay behind or there'd be nobody to turn the key.

"Who'll try it first?" Patrick was asking.

Omri looked at him. "Are you serious? You really want to try it?"

"Of course! Don't you?"

Omri looked around the room. Despite irritations, he was happy with it, with his life. He wasn't eager to risk losing either of them.

"Have you thought about the dangers?"

"Coward!"

"No I'm not. You're rushing in like you always do. Just stop and think a bit. First, if it does work at all, how can you be sure you'd go back to Little Bear's time, to his village, and not somewhere else? You could find yourself anywhere. And any *when*." Patrick looked mulish. "Apart from that, what about size?"

"Size?"

"Yes. If *they* reach us small, we'd reach them small. Wouldn't we? Of course there was no plastic then. We'd have to be in dolls or—totem poles or something. I don't think it's cowardly not to fancy waking up in an Indian village two hundred years ago, at the top of a totem pole."

For answer, Patrick knelt down by the chest and started lifting things out of it. "Give me a hand with all this rubbish" was all he said.

Omri helped him silently until the chest was empty. Then he said, "After all that, probably the key won't even fit this lock." His heart was pounding and he knew he hoped it wouldn't.

Patrick got up and fetched the key. Without closing the lid of the chest, he put it in the lock and turned it. It turned easily. The lock part clicked. Patrick removed the key and looked at it.

"My guess is, this key fits pretty well any lock," he said slowly.

Omri took a deep breath. Once again, he was caught up in something he felt overwhelmed by.

"Who'll go first?"

"I will," said Patrick.

"Wait a minute!"

"What *now*?"

"You've got to have something with you, something of Little Bear's. Otherwise you haven't a hope of finishing up in the right place!"

Patrick stopped. "What have we got of his?"

"The longhouse."

"That's no use. The longhouse was made here; he didn't bring it from his time."

"Then, there's only the tepee."

They looked over at Omri's desk. The tiny tepee stood up from the seed tray, its poles sticking through the top, its beautiful bold animal designs on its cone-shaped panels.

"That came from somewhere else. The Iroquois didn't

have tepees, only longhouses. Besides, we can't move that. Bright Stars is having her baby in it."

Patrick said slowly, "If I took *her*, I'd be sure to go back to the right place. She'd take me."

"Patrick, you can't! Take her back into the middle of a battle?"

"Listen, it's her village, it's her place. If not for the accident of you bringing them when you did, she'd be there now. I bet it's where she'd rather be, if you asked her— didn't you see how she was begging Little Bear just before he left?"

"But he wanted—"

"Listen, shut up! You're always arguing. I've made up my mind. I'm not going to miss this chance. I want to see the battle. Don't let's have a fight over it or somebody's sure to get hurt. And it might not be one of us."

He went to the desk and fetched the seed tray and brought it back and laid it carefully in the bottom of the chest. Omri watched, feeling terribly agitated. He wanted to fight Patrick, but that was impossible now—he should have done it earlier. Now if they started struggling something awful could happen to Boone or Bright Stars.

His mind was racing. "I'm the one who'll have the key," he thought. He would have control. He could send them for five minutes, or one minute, or less, and then, just by turning the key in the lock again, he could recover them.

That was how it worked. What could happen in such a short time? And he couldn't help admiring Patrick's courage. Omri admitted to himself that he would not have been willing to go first, and not just because of Bright Stars, either.

Patrick climbed into the chest and crouched down.

"Here," he said, handing Omri the key. "Close the lid and send me."

"Touch the tepee with one finger," said Omri.

"Okay, I am. Now." Patrick's voice was trembling a little, but not much.

"What about Boone?"

"He said he felt bad and wanted to help. Send us, will you, before I lose my nerve!"

Omri closed down the lid, put the key in the lock, and locked the chest.

It was such a simple action. What had it caused?

After a moment he unlocked the chest again, and, with icy cold hands, opened it. He didn't know what to expect. Would Patrick have disappeared?

Patrick lay inside it. At least, his body lay there. Omri reached in and touched him. He felt cold.

"Patrick! *Patrick!*" But he was not really expecting a response. Patrick was as far away as anyone can be who isn't actually dead.

Down in the bottom of the chest, near Patrick's unconscious head, was the seed tray. Patrick's limp hand was resting on it. Everything else on it was the same—the grass patch, the longhouse, the pool—except for one thing. The tepee was made of plastic. The paintings on it were crude, mass-produced; the poles were pink and molded in one with the tent. Gently Omri lifted it. What he saw underneath gave him the biggest shock he'd had yet.

The plastic figure of an Indian girl lay on a pile of cotton bedding. A cowboy was kneeling by her on one knee. In his arms was a tiny naked plastic baby, smaller than Omri's little fingernail.

Omri gasped. Then, on an impulse, he reached in and lifted the seed tray and its contents out of the chest. Then he slammed down the lid and turned the key. About half a minute had passed since he had "sent" Patrick. At once he heard him moving inside and threw back the lid.

Patrick raised his head. His face was white and dazed.

"Don't!" he gasped.

"What happened?" shouted Omri.

"I'd hardly got there! It's fantastic—listen—I was part of the tepee!"

"What-at!"

"I can't explain! I was in the tepee—not in it—I *was* it! I was on the outside of it—I could see everything! The place is—it's—I hadn't time to look properly, I could just—Send me back, will you? Send me back *now*!"

He reached up and tried to pull down the lid. But Omri

braced himself against it.

"Get out. It's my turn."

"You didn't even want to go—"

"Well, I do now."

Omri was almost unable to speak for excitement. He was trying to drag Patrick bodily out of the chest.

Patrick, resisting, grated out, "Leave off! Listen—I heard a baby crying in the tepee—"

"I know. It's Bright Stars's. Get *out*, will you?—Were you small—?"

"I don't know how big I was, but I couldn't move— Listen, it's not fair, let me go back, let me stay for a bit, you hardly let me—"

"I've got to see!" Omri said frenziedly. "Let me just look! Give me five minutes, by your watch, then you can have five, I swear—"

Patrick gave way. He changed places with Omri.

"You'd better take the tepee—"

"The tepee won't work now, all that will happen is, you'll bring them back. I've got her moccasins in my pocket. Those ought to do. Go on, get on with it!"

"Five minutes!" said Patrick, and locked the chest.

There wasn't a second in which to catch a breath or even feel scared. Omri was curled in the dark innards of the chest, he heard the lock click, and then, immediately, he felt sunlight shining on him. He tried to open his eyes but found they were already open—at any rate he could see. And he could hear. That was all he could do. He not only couldn't move, he couldn't try to move; but he didn't feel uncomfortable or as if he were tied up. He just had nothing to move *with* and that was that.

Spread out before him was a ruined Indian village. It was evening. The sun was a red ball sinking toward the rocky edge of a hill. The village was in a clearing in a forest of pine and maple trees. The maples were all the colors of fire. It was as if the fires in the village, which had now burnt out, had kindled more fires in the surrounding woods.

There were few longhouses left standing. Many had been burnt to the ground. They had stopped smoldering but their blackened ruins gave the view a look of desolation. A number of women were moving about. Some were carrying water, some were cooking, others were helping injured men. There were Indian children of all ages, and quite a few dogs. Hardly any young men.

Omri could see no signs of anything resembling a battle. What had become of the troop of well-armed Indians they'd dispatched less than an hour ago? Had they gotten lost on the way . . . ?

Suddenly he heard a sound from behind him. It was unmistakably the strange, chuckling cry of a newborn baby. Omri tried to look round but found that he couldn't.

Whatever he was, he was stuck to the outside of the tepee, and that meant he couldn't see in.

A very queer and comic thought came to him.

"I wonder if I'm the beaver or the porcupine?"

He didn't have time to consider this before he heard Boone's voice.

"He sure is a fine li'l fella," he said. His voice was choked with emotion. "Ever'thin' jest whur it oughta be. Now you give him a swig o' milk, ma'am, an' Ah'll go ask the boys fer somethin' fer you, t'give ya back your stren'th."

There was a movement to Omri's left and Boone came into view, blowing his nose and wiping his eyes. Amazingly, he was full size. Or, no, of course that wasn't amazing at all.

"A fine li'l fella," he was muttering to himself, sniffing and shaking his head. "Gee whiz, ain't nature wonderful! Ah kin hardly—"

He stopped dead and stared around him in horrified astonishment.

"Holy jumpin' catfish! Whur am Ah?"

Omri was aching to tell him, but he could no more talk than he could move. However, Boone was no fool. He realized soon enough what had happened. After a few seconds spent taking in the scene, he turned and dived back into the tepee. Fortunately, no one seemed to have seen him.

"Hey, li'l lady, do you know whur we're at? Ah do believe we're in yor village! No, no—now, don't you go gittin' up—gee, I shouldn't oughta've told ya—"

A moment later, Bright Stars emerged, her baby in her arms. She looked tired and a bit bedraggled, but otherwise fine. Beautiful. Omri, who had only seen her tiny till now, had never appreciated how beautiful she was.

An Indian woman was passing. She noticed Bright Stars, and reacted to the baby. She called to others. Soon there was a crowd of women around Bright Stars, much chattering talk, and a lot of pointing, all westward toward the setting sun. Omri hoped Boone would have sense enough to stay in the tepee, and he did. After a minute or two, Bright Stars moved to go back in. Several of the other women wanted to come with her, but she sent them away.

Now Omri strained to hear the conversation in the tepee behind him.

"Whut's goin' on?" asked Boone as soon as she reentered.

"Woman say, strange thing happen. Little Bear come with many brave. Go to hills. Wait for new attack."

"Whut attack?" asked Boone in alarm.

"Soldier maybe not come back. Algonquin come. Take women, food, furs."

"They didn't git any loot when they come last time?"

"No. Iroquois fight, drive off. Algonquin burn, kill some, get nothing. Now village wait. Little Bear wait in hills. Algonquin come back when sun go."

"But the sun's almost gone now!" said Boone, his voice going squeaky.

"Yes," said Bright Stars quietly.

After a moment, Boone's voice said, "Ain't ya skeered? With yer baby an' all?" Bright Stars didn't answer. After a while she said, "Little Bear near. And Great Spirits. No bad come."

Omri's eyes—or the porcupine's, or the beaver's, whosever he was looking through—were fixed on the sun. It was sinking behind the rocky hillside so fast he could see it move. Only a jagged slice of it was left. Darkness was coming, and his five minutes was more than up. Why hadn't Patrick taken him back?

18

Algonquin

T HERE WAS AN AIR of fear about the village. As twilight fell, the villagers seemed to be preparing to decamp. Such men as were left—mainly old, plus some wounded or unfit ones—were giving orders, and the women were running here and there, packing things into bundles. Others came with buckets of water and put out the few cooking fires that were burning, removed the pots and rounded up the children. A few dogs were dashing about, barking excitedly, sensing something in the hurrying and the anxious voices.

Omri watched all this in growing alarm. The minutes were ticking by. Being apparently nothing more than a picture on the side of a tepee, he couldn't see how he could be in danger himself, but he was desperately worried about Bright Stars, Boone and the baby.

After a while, one of the old women came around the tepee into Omri's sight. She was hobbling along as fast as she could, gazing up at the tepee with gaping mouth as if it had dropped from nowhere (as, in a way, it had). She bent at the flap and called. Bright Stars answered. The old woman hobbled away again, her white hair glowing in the deep twilight. The tall pines around the camp now stood out black against the darkening sky.

Omri heard Bright Stars in the tepee say to Boone: "Village leave now."

"Whut's that? Leave fur where?"

"Hide in wood." There was a pause. Then she said doubtfully, "Boone come?"

"No. Ah cain't."

"Why no? Here not safe."

"*There* not safe! Not fur me. Ah don't fit in, gal. You know that."

Bright Stars said no more. There was a pause; then the tepee flap opened and she came out with her baby wrapped up in some hide torn from her skirt. She turned in the opening. There was a very soft look in her eyes as she looked, presumably at Boone, standing out of Omri's sight inside. Then she hurried away, mingling with the knot of other Indians in the center of the village.

Soon they were forming into a rough procession. It was almost too dark to see now, but Omri could just make them out as they silently made their way out of the circle of ruined and half-burnt buildings. Even the dogs were quiet now as they trailed along after the villagers. One of them, lingering, passed the tepee. He paused to leave his mark against the side of it, and for a moment he looked up, straight at Omri. His lips drew back over teeth which shone white in the darkness and he whined uneasily—the hair on his back stood up straight. Then he tucked his long tail between his legs and shot off after the others.

Soon the last rustles and murmurs subsided and there was a deep silence, broken only by the call of a single owl. Bird—or a signal?

Omri had never known real fear. All he could compare this with was walking up Hovel Road and knowing he had to pass the skinheads who were waiting for him. That seemed to him now like nothing at all. What was the worst they could do to him, after all? A black eye, a few bruises? This was in another category of fear altogether.

Yet, what was he afraid of? Nothing could happen to *him*. At any second now, Patrick would turn the key in the lock of the chest and recall him to his body, to normality, to the utter, blissful safety of his own life, which he had never thought about before, far less appreciated.

So what was this icy feeling which could only be terror?

Perhaps it was for Boone. Boone was behind him in the tepee, no longer a tiny figure, but a full-sized man, out of his place, out of his time. Visible, solid, vulnerable, and quite alone. How lonely could you be? Omri could hardly imagine how Boone must be feeling as he waited in the tepee for some unknown thing to happen.

And suddenly it did.

It began with another hoot from the owl. Then Omri saw a swift movement to one side of him, close to the edge of the clearing. Then again, on the other side. Then a man's figure, crouched low, scurried past him. And abruptly the whole clearing seemed to be full of moving men.

They were not Frenchmen, of course. They were

Indians. Little Bear's men, returning to defend the place? Omri strained to see them. All he could make out was glimpses of leggings, of a head feather—the flash of an axhead catching the starlight. Then he saw that several men were raking wood from the cooking fires into one heap in the center of the ring of longhouses. Shadows began to spread from a light source in the midst of the men. Suddenly a flame leapt high, and another. The fire had been lit. And at once Omri could see.

These weren't Little Bear's men! Their clothes were different. Their heads were shaved. Their headdresses—even their movements—were alien. Their faces, too—their faces! They were wild, distorted, terrifying masks of hatred and rage.

They were Algonquins, come to sack the village.

In the light of the central fire, they ran to and fro, dozens of them—scores. It took only moments to find out that they had been outwitted, that the village was empty and there was nothing to steal, no women to carry off. Their anger burst out in howls and yelps. Through this outburst Omri heard a smothered groan below him. Boone! . . . he must be peering out at the awful scene.

Now the Indians were dipping branches into the big fire to make torches. They were dancing and shouting and leaping. Several of them were running to the few unburnt longhouses. And suddenly Omri knew.

He knew what he had feared. They were going to burn the tepee. And he was part of it!

The tepee was on the edge of the clearing. There were other things to set on fire first. But they would get to him! They were coming closer, their howls fiercer, their torches swirling in clouds of smoke above their half-naked heads.

Omri began screaming silently.

Patrick! Patrick! Do it now! Turn the key, bring me home, save me!

He saw an Indian making straight for him. His face, in the torchlight, was twisted with fury. For a second Omri saw, under the shaven scalp decorated with a single scalp lock, the mindless destructive face of a skinhead just before he lashed out. The torch went back with the man's right arm, there was a split second's pause, and then it came hurtling through the air and struck the panel of hide just beside Omri.

It slithered down to the ground and lay there, its flame chewing the bottom edge. The Algonquin licked his lips, snarling like the dog, and ran back to the central fire.

Omri had not realized he could smell as well as see and hear. Now he smelt the smoke, the stench of burning hide. It was dry and it caught quickly. In helpless horror Omri watched the burnt area growing up beside him like the letter A edged with flame. He hardly noticed another Indian approaching from the other side with another blazing brand until suddenly, out of the daze of fear he had fallen into, Omri heard a loud bang.

The Indian left the ground briefly. His fingers jerked open. The torch fell. Then the man did the same, dropped like a stone, and lay motionless on his back while the branch burnt harmlessly beside him.

All the others stopped dead, their grim faces turned toward the tepee.

The shot had come from below. Omri saw the tip of a revolver barrel poking out of a slit in the hide just underneath him. And as the whole pack of Algonquin began to run, howling and yelling, toward the tepee, their monstrous shadows sliding along the ground ahead of them, more shots rang out, and two, then three more Indians fell.

The others hesitated, then scattered. The fire burnt clear in the center, unattended. The fire that was eating the tepee burnt too. Inside, behind him, Omri could hear and even feel Boone frantically beating at the licking flames with something—his hat, perhaps—and cursing. But it was useless. The fire was spreading.

Get out, Boone! Run, Boone, run into the forest, save yourself!

Smoke flowed past the painted animal Omri was inhabiting and blinded him.

19

The Terror of the Battle

FROM THE DARK HEART of the fear, Omri heard a new sound.

He could see nothing now. But through the snapping of the flames, which were already licking at him, came a sudden deafening rattle.

Then isolated bangs. Nearer and nearer. With no other warning, something exploded almost under him. The tepee crashed to its side. Omri felt it on top of him. The fire noise stopped and so did the smoke, though the smell was still there. The falling tepee had put the flames out. There was a sensation of heaviness, then of threshing, and he could hear Boone's rich cursing as he struggled to get out of the crumpled, half-burnt folds of the tent.

In his struggles, he turned the whole thing over. Now Omri was staring up at the night sky. He could see the stars, with smoke drifting close above him, and the reflection of the central bonfire on a few pine tops.

A cowboy boot loomed for a second against the starlight, and came down, narrowly missing Omri. Boone stood above him, astride him, firing into the surrounding darkness once, twice. "Take that, ya flea-bitten coyote!" he yelled. Then a click . . . Omri found he had been counting. That was the sixth, and last, bullet.

The rattle came again, closer, and Boone flung himself down on the fallen tepee—on Omri. Omri could smell his sweat now, feel how his heart was thundering through his shirt, hear him muttering a mixture of curses and prayers . . . The machine-gun bullets whizzed overhead. There was the numbing crash of another hand grenade exploding somewhere near the big fire.

Now, to the noise of explosions, were added shrieks and screams of terror, and other shouts, war cries, as Little Bear's men descended from ambush onto the hapless Algonquins. Omri heard the thunder of a single pair of hoofs drumming on the ground beneath him. Boone rolled aside, and at almost the same moment the stars were blotted out as the pony cleared tepee, Boone and all in a wild leap. As it galloped on, Omri caught a glimpse of Little Bear on its back, waving a rifle above his head, riding down three fleeing Algonquins.

The noise of the firing was now continuous and deafening. Omri could see the flash of large and small explosions in the dark. The tide of the battle swept to and fro chaotically. Twice or three times, small groups of Indians—whether friends or enemies, Omri couldn't tell—raced across the fallen tent. One tripped over Boone and went flying. His bare foot scraped Omri's face.

It was the nightmare to end nightmares. Utterly powerless, unable to move or escape or fight back or even close his eyes and ears, Omri had long since stopped hoping that some miracle would save him. He had totally forgotten Patrick, forgotten his other life. He was a helpless witness to the chaos and carnage of war; he was part of it, yet not part of it. It seemed it would go on forever, or until some kind of oblivion engulfed him . . .

Then, in the tenth part of a second, it ended.

The noise, the smoke, the cries—the terror—the helplessness. Gone . . .

Silence.

He lay curled up in darkness on something hard. He could feel his body, his wonderful, three-dimensional body . . . Light fell on him, and warm air. And he heard Patrick's voice, with panic in it, calling his name.

He lifted himself slowly. One hand clutched the edge of the chest. The other went to the right side of his face.

Patrick was staring at him, aghast, as if he saw a stranger.

"God, Omri! Are you all right?"

Omri didn't answer. The side of his head felt funny. He took his hand away and some black stuff was on his fingers. Something was odd about his nose, too. He felt something running out of it. He looked down. There was blood on his sweatshirt.

"What's happened to you? You look—your nose is bleeding, and your hair—!"

None of that mattered. The blood and the singed and blackened hair meant nothing. They didn't give him any pain or any fear, at least none that he would call fear now. Stiffly Omri crawled out of the chest, trying to get his mind back together, to clear it and to adjust.

Patrick was babbling something about Omri's mother.

"She just came in, I couldn't do anything, she made me go downstairs to the phone, and then she wouldn't let me go back up again—she kept asking where you were, she delayed me, I was going crazy, she wouldn't let me go . . . Omri, I'm sorry, you look terrible, as if you'd nearly been killed or something—what happened? Is it over? Should we bring the others back?"

Omri had a pad of something pressed to his nose. His head, where the fire had licked, was beginning to sting. It was awfully hard to think. He remembered what Boone had said about Little Bear, and kept repeating to himself: *Pore critter's had a shock. Pore critter* . . . The "poor creature" was himself.

The others . . . He turned suddenly.

"Get Boone back!" he shouted. "Not the others, but get Boone! Hurry!"

Patrick snatched up the plastic tepee, and Boone's figure from under it.

"Don't forget his hat!" Omri said idiotically. Patrick scrabbled about in the earth of the seed tray, and almost threw it after the figure and the tent. He slammed down the lid of the chest, turned the key . . .

"If only he's not dead . . ." breathed Omri. His head was beginning to ache piercingly from the burnt side. Patrick threw up the lid again.

They looked down into the belly of the chest. The tepee was a crumpled wreck, twisted and blackened. Boone lay on top of it. He was very still. For one horrible moment, Omri thought a stray bullet or the blast from an explosion must have killed him. But then he raised his red head and looked up at them.

"Is it over?" he called.

"It's over for us, Boone," said Omri.

Gently he lifted him out.

"Wuz you there too? Whur was ya, son?"

"You were lying on me part of the time," said Omri.

Boone didn't try to puzzle this out.

"Dang me if'n it wuzn't the most fearsomest thing Ah

ever bin through in mah en-tire life!"

"Me, too," said Omri soberly.

Patrick was staring at them. "Have I missed it?" he said. "Is it over?"

"I don't know," said Omri.

With a sudden movement, Patrick leapt into the chest.

"What are you doing?" cried Omri, although he knew.

"Send me back! I've missed everything, and you've seen it! Send me back—"

"No."

"You've got to! It's only fair."

"Never mind fair. You don't know what you're talking about. It was . . . Never mind that you missed it. You're lucky."

"But—"

"It's no use. I wouldn't send you now for a million pounds."

Patrick saw he meant it, and when he looked at Omri's face, brave as he was he couldn't really be sorry.

He climbed slowly out again. "Tell me about everything," he said.

Omri told him, with Boone chipping in. Boone had accounted for three, possibly four Indians before he ran "plumb outa bullets."

"You'd better do something about that burn," Patrick said at the end.

"Yeah . . . What, though?"

"You're going to have to let your mum see it some-time."

"How'll I explain it? And my nosebleed?"

Patrick said the nosebleed was nothing—"We could have had a fight." The burn was the problem. Half the hair on that side of his head was gone and there was a big red blister.

"Well, you don't have to worry about explaining it now," said Patrick. "They've gone out."

"Who?"

"Your lot, your parents and your brothers."

"Is the baby-sitter here?"

"Not yet, she's late. Can you cope till morning?"

Omri didn't know. He supposed so. He was ashamed to admit how his heart had sunk when Patrick said his mother wasn't in the house. He suddenly wanted her. He wanted to tell her everything and let her take care of it, and him. Well, he couldn't, that was all. Just as well, perhaps.

Boone, exhausted, flopped down in the longhouse for a sleep, after flinging back the last of the whiskey. Patrick and Omri slipped down to the next-floor bathroom and found some ointment, which Omri rubbed on his own head. The sight of himself in the mirror scared him silly. His face was white, red and black. He felt he could be doing with some whiskey himself, but he made do with an aspirin.

"What about the others?" asked Patrick.

"I don't know."

Omri felt the whole thing had gone well beyond his control. Having seen Boone, Little Bear and Bright Stars full size, he could no longer think of them in the same way. Some part of him—until the battle—had still thought of them as "his," not toys exactly, but belonging to him, within his orbit. This illusion was now gone. What was happening back in the village? Whatever it was, he was responsible for it. He couldn't avoid the realization that he had sent devastating modern weapons back in time and that they had certainly killed people. "Baddies," of course . . . But who were baddies? If Patrick, a year ago, had made him a present of some other plastic Indian, it might just as well have been an Algonquin, and then the Iroquois would have been the baddies. Suddenly Omri felt the nightmare was not there, but here.

"I think we should bring them back," said Patrick.

"Bring them back if you want to," said Omri, who suddenly felt tired to death. "I've got to sleep." He started back up the stairs to his room, and stopped. Not up there. He wanted . . . neutral ground. He turned and went down again.

"Where are you going?" asked Patrick.

"Down to the living room. I'm going to sleep on the sofa."

"What when the baby-sitter comes?"

"Shove her in the breakfast room." He stopped, and met Patrick's eyes. "Don't do anything stupid," he said. "I really can't cope with any more."

"I'll take care of everything," said Patrick.

Omri went on, his feet like lead weights. In the living room he didn't even put the light on, just threw himself onto the sofa, where in two minutes he was fast asleep.

20

Invasion

H**E SLEPT WITHOUT** dreams for two hours. Then something woke him.

He lifted his head sharply. His mother hadn't closed the curtains so a little light came in from the street. He felt strange but he saw at once where he was and remembered why he was there. He was by no means ready to wake up— so why had he?

Then he saw there was somebody in the room.

Coming in, rather. Through an open window, facing the front garden, which shouldn't have been open. It was the sound of it opening, and the draught of cold night air, which had awakened him. He was peering over the arm of the sofa, which lay in deep shadow at the farthest end of the living room. He could see the clear silhouette of a male figure stealthily putting first one leg and then the other over the sill, and ducking his head under the half-raised window frame. A bare head, which gleamed dully in the diffused lamplight from beyond the high front hedge.

For a second, Omri thought it was an Algonquin. But there was no scalp lock on that shaven skull. It was a skin-head. No—not just one. Once in, the first figure bent and beckoned, and from the shadows outside appeared another, and then another. One by one they climbed silently into Omri's house.

In a flash he remembered last night (was it only last night?) when he'd come down to fetch Bright Stars something to eat. He'd seen a hairless head go past the kitchen window, and then put it from his mind. They must have been looking the place over, "casing the joint," making plans for a time when the family would be out . . .

Where was the baby-sitter?

Normally she would be in here, watching television. But the set sat darkling in its corner. The intruders made towards it, laid hands on it. While one unplugged it and rolled up the cord, the other two lifted it between them. Would they try to take it out by the window . . . ? No. They carried it silently to the door. The cord holder opened it and they went out.

Omri swung his legs swiftly to the floor and stood up, holding his breath. His heartbeat was extraordinarily steady; in fact he felt calm and clear-headed. There was another door to the living room, and it was the one nearest the foot of the stairs. Moving across the carpet without a sound, he slipped out of the room and glanced toward the front door.

It was open. The skinheads were going down the path, but they weren't yet ready to make off. They put the television down in the front garden just behind the hedge. Omri knew they would then turn and come back for more. He took two swift steps to the stairs and raced up them silently, two at a time.

He must phone the police.

No, he couldn't. The only phone was in the hall.

He must do *something*. He couldn't just let them get away with it. It was bad enough they made his life a hell in Hovel Road, without invading his territory. But the inescapable fact was that they were years older than Omri, there were three of them, they probably had knives.

He reached his attic bedroom out of breath and opened the door as quietly as he could. He stopped. It was full of strange small lights and flickering shadows.

The first thing he saw was Patrick, fast asleep on cushions on the floor. Then he noticed that the cupboard had been returned to the top of the chest, and so had the seed tray. There seemed to be a lot of activity going on on its much-trampled earth surface. Omri moved forward to look closer.

An astonishing scene met his eyes.

The ruined longhouse had been turned into a sort of scratch hospital. Clean pages evidently torn from a notebook had been laid on the floor. In a double row, with a walkway between their feet, lay a number of wounded Indians. They appeared to have been well looked after. The ones Omri could see, through the holes in the long-house roof, were bandaged and covered with warm blankets, made of squares cut from Omri's sports socks—he recognized the green and blue stripes on the white toweling. Bright Stars was there, her baby tied to her back, moving among them with a bucket, giving them drinks.

At either end of the building burned a small fire of matchsticks and shavings of candlewax, each tended by an unwounded Indian. Around the fires, wrapped in glove-finger sacks, more braves lay asleep.

Omri's eyes went to a bright light at one end of the seed tray. The stub of the candle had been stuck into the earth and lit. Around it, muttering and chanting, Little Bear moved in a slow sort of dance. His shadow, hugely enlarged, was flung all over the walls of Omri's room, and the thin, weird, wailing note of his chant struck Omri's heart with sadness.

Near the candle was the paddock. It was like a grave-yard. Laid out on the grass were some small, still shapes, covered with squares of white cotton blotted with drops of red. Omri counted them. There were eight. Eight out of forty. And all those injured. How?—when they had ambushed the unsuspecting enemy, with far superior weapons?

It took only a few seconds for Omri to take all this in. Then, out of the depths of the longhouse, bustled a little figure in blue and white, with a tall, flowing cap.

"Well!" she exclaimed when she saw him. "Here's a nice how do y' do! Call this a casualty ward? I'd rather be Florence Nightingale—*she* had it easy! Whoever let these poor, simple fools loose with modern weapons ought to be shot themselves!"

"What happened?" asked Omri, dry-mouthed.

"What was bound to happen. *They were shooting each other!* From what I can make out from their leader, they encircled the enemy, then blasted off from all sides, never realizing how far the bullets would travel. The shots that didn't hit an enemy were likely to hit an ally coming the other way! I've fished so many bullets out tonight I could do it with my eyes shut . . ." She bustled back to work, tutting loudly.

Omri bent and shook Patrick awake.

"Get up. We've got burglars downstairs."

Patrick jerked upright. "What!"

"Skinheads. Three of them. They must think the house is empty. They're going to clean us out. Only, they're not, because we're going to stop them."

"We are? How?"

"Where are the guns the Indians had?"

"They're in the cupboard. I think they've damaged a lot of them."

"We were mad . . . Where's that bag of British soldiers we had in the garden?"

"Here—but you're not going—"

"And where's Fickits?"

"He's in with them."

Omri was frantically emptying the paper bag onto the chest. He found Fickits at once and almost threw him into the cupboard, remembering just in time to take the jumble of rifles, tommy guns and machine guns out first. He locked and unlocked the door, and in the next moment Fickits was standing bewildered by the pile of guns.

"Corporal! Check those weapons."

Fickits, rubbing his eyes, at once came to attention, and then began disentangling what now appeared to be a pile of scrap. Omri meanwhile was putting handfuls of soldiers recklessly into the cupboard. Patrick was at his shoulder.

"You're crazy! You're always telling me not to—"

"Shut up and bring me something flat."

"Like what—?"

Omri turned on him fiercely. "Use your head! Anything! A tray, a book! My loose-leaf will do! Be quick!"

Patrick did as he was told. Omri closed the cupboard but didn't turn the key.

"Corporal!"

"Yessir?"

"How much ammo is left?"

"Ammo, sir? More like, how many workin' weapons. Them redskins 'ave wreaked 'avoc, sir. Absolute 'avoc. I was afraid of this, sir. These 'ere are precision instruments, sir, they're not bloomin' bows an' arrers!"

"Never mind that now. I'm going to put you in charge of a—an operation, Fickits."

"Me, sir?"

"—Not Indians this time; British troops. And they're going to mount an attack on three people my size."

"Gawd 'elp us, sir! 'Ow can we?"

"Just do as I tell you, Corporal, and make them do as you tell them. Okay?"

Fickits gulped noisily, then straightened himself.

"As long as most of 'em are Marines, sir, I expect we shall manage."

"Good man! Stand by to reassure them as they come out."

174

"No need for mollycoddling 'em, sir. The light's poor; I'll just tell 'em we're on night maneuvers."

Omri turned the key in the lock, and opened the door at once. He was glad the light in the room was dim. Patrick thrust Omri's large, flat loose-leaf book in front of the cupboard, and out onto it poured twenty or thirty tiny khaki-clad figures. Some of them still had their weapons; others, obeying Fickits's barking orders, began to man some of those the Indians had used. The room filled with the metallic sounds of weapons being loaded.

"Shall we use the big guns this time, sir? Now we've got the crews?" Fickits asked Omri aside.

"Yes. Marshal them all on here, and tell the men to prepare for an all-out attack when you give the word."

"No trouble, sir. Just don't—er—" He coughed. "Don't thrust yourself forward, sir. They 'aven't spotted anything unusual yet, if you take my meaning."

Patrick had caught the spirit of the thing and was feverishly sorting out every bit of hardware he could find in the biscuit tin and getting the cupboard and key to work on it. Soon the men, who were armed with light arms, machine guns, portable antitank rockets, and even a "bunker-buster"—a Milan missile—were in position, drawn up on three sides of a square with their backs to Omri. Though this was a formidable array, Omri did not feel even the faintest scruple.

"Fickets," he whispered, "I'm going to transport you all. When you can see your targets, give the order to fire at will!"

"Sir!"

"And don't worry! Nobody's going to get hurt."

"You hope," muttered Patrick as they started down the darkened stairs.

21

Battle of the Skinheads

THEY MOVED SILENTLY down through the darkness. Omri could feel, through his hands holding the edges of the loose-leaf platform, the faint vibrations of life. He could also, for the first time since it happened, feel the sting where the row of minute bullets had pierced the skin of his palm.

On the first landing he nudged Patrick to a stop.

Low down on the bottom flight of stairs was one which always creaked. He heard it creak now. He changed direction and slipped through a half-open door into the bathroom.

He and Patrick stood behind this door. There was

another door to this room, which led into his parents' bedroom, and it, too, was ajar. They saw a faint light—the sort made by a penlight—feeling its way about on the landing, and heard the stealthy sounds of the skinheads following it. Then a faint whisper:

"Let's try in 'ere—"

The finger of light vanished, to appear again through the other door. The intruders were in Omri's parents' room. He could hear them moving furtively about, then the soft whine of a wardrobe opening.

"Gaaah—no fur coats . . ."

Omri and Patrick stood rooted, hardly breathing. Omri was almost praying that, in the darkness, no soldier would press a trigger by mistake. Suddenly the torchlight was within two feet of them on the other side of the door.

"Look 'ere, Kev! . . ."

Omri set his teeth. He knew what they'd found. A little oak chest with small, shallow drawers in which his mother kept the few bits of jewelry she owned, most of it old silver inherited from her mother. It was very precious to her, though it wasn't specially valuable. Omri heard the scrape of the wooden drawers, and then:

"We can flog this lot . . . Let's just take the 'ole thing—"

And then another voice, farther away but audible because they thought they were safe and were getting careless:

"'Ere! I'm goin' to take a leak on their bed—"

And there was a burst of stifled sniggering.

That did it.

Before Omri could even signal, Patrick had let out a growl of disgust and flung the door open.

"The light-switch! Beside you!" Omri shouted.

There was an agonizing second while Patrick groped. Then the top light came on, flooding the bedroom with brightness. The skinheads froze in grotesque positions, like children playing statues. Their ugly faces were turned toward the boys, their eyes popping, their loose mouths gaping.

Omri rushed in like an avenging fury, and stopped, the loose-leaf platform with its contingent of men thrust out in front of him.

"'Ere, wot the 'ell—"

Then Fickits's sergeant-major voice rang shrill and clear: "FIRE AT WILL!"

The biggest skinhead snarled and made a dive towards Omri. For a split second he loomed menacingly. Then there was a concerted burst of fire, and suddenly tiny red spots appeared on his face in a line, from the bottom of one cheek, diagonally across his nose to the top of the other. He stopped dead in his tracks, let out a howl of pain and outrage, and clapped his hands to his face.

"I bin stung! It's 'ornets! Get 'em orfa me!"

Behind him, his mate started towards Patrick, hands reaching out to grab.

"I'll get 'em—little nerds—"

But all he got was the miniature equivalent of an armor-piercing shell up under his thumbnail.

"OWWW!" he shrieked, and let out a string of curses, shaking his hand and dancing in agony.

The third and smallest of the gang had been gazing at the object Omri held, and he, unlike the others, had *seen*. He now let out a sound that started as a moan and ended in a scream.

"UughhhhhAAAOWEEEE!"

He then flew into a panic, dashing here and there in short spurts, yelling, "'Elp! They're alive, I seen 'em, they're alive!"—through the crump and crack and chatter of the guns, which were firing continuously. The other two also turned and tried to flee, but all sense of direction had deserted them. They bumped into the furniture, the walls and each other, swearing and howling, and giving great leaps into the air every time they were hit in a sensitive spot. Omri and Patrick added to the uproar by shouting encouragement to their little men. Patrick was jumping about as if at a prizefight or a football match. Omri had to stay still to hold the firing platform steady, but he opened his throat on a long shout of excitement as the three invaders finally found the other exit and fled through it, pell-mell.

"Cease fire!" cried Patrick.

"CEASE FIRE!" bawled Fickits.

There was a fraction of a second's silence. Then the boys heard the skinheads shoving and swearing on the stairs. One of them tripped; there was a series of satisfying thumps, and then a loud crack as one of the banisters broke. The boys, hurrying down to the half landing, saw them fleeing along the path and heard the clatter of their boots receding along Hovel Road, accompanied by sounds of anguish.

The boys turned and hugged each other.

"We did it, we did it!"

"The way you switched the light on—terrific!"

"How you could hold that thing straight—I'd have tipped them all off, I was so excited!—Hey! Where is it?"

"I put it on the bed—"

They rushed back into the bedroom. Fickits was calmly ordering the men to clear up and cover the big guns.

When he noticed the boys, he left the men and edged to the back of the platform.

"Operation a success, sir?" he asked in a quiet tone.

"Definitely, Fickits. Well done!" said Omri.

"Did I say a sergeant, Fickits?" said Patrick. "I meant a captain."

"Not me, sir! Too much responsibility." He coughed. "Better get the men fell in and back to quarters as quick as possible, sir."

"Yeah, right," said Patrick. "Thanks again, Corporal, it was terrific." And he started to carry them upstairs.

"See that everything's all right up there," said Omri.

"Okay." Patrick reached the door and stopped. "I don't mind so much now, missing the other battle," he said. "Wasn't this one *fantastic*?"

"Yeah," said Omri.

He was thinking how fantastic it was, too, that he would never be afraid to walk down Hovel Road again. They would leave him severely alone from now on, and even if they didn't . . . Having sent them flying like that, and after all he'd been through tonight, he couldn't imagine them holding any terrors for him in the future.

He looked around the room. He was going to have a bit of explaining to do. The glass on a picture was cracked, and there were a number of pinholes, and some larger ones, in the wallpaper and the foot of the bed . . . Then there was the banister. And his own injuries . . . Well, he could tell his parents about the burglars, say there was a scuffle. Maybe they'd believe it. He hoped so.

He bent and picked his mother's jewel box up off its

face. He'd saved that for her, anyway. Under it was a cheap penlight. He picked it up. It was still lit. He switched it off and dropped it into his pocket. He might, if he felt like it, just hand it back to that little skinhead, if he bumped into him after school on Monday . . . Be a good laugh, to see his face.

Omri drew a deep breath of satisfaction and went downstairs to bring in the stuff piled in the front garden.

Epilogue by the Fire

WHEN EVERYTHING was back in place, with Patrick's help, except the banister rail, which needed gluing in three places, they made some hot chocolate to take upstairs with some cold potatoes and other leftovers. They were both so keyed up they couldn't feel their tiredness, and were prepared to sit up all night.

"I sent Matron back for some drugs and stuff she wanted," Patrick said. "But she made me promise I'd get her again in the morning. She says she's going to take a week's leave from St. Thomas's . . . She's enjoyed all this, anyway."

"Fickits, too."

"Little Bear hasn't enjoyed it."

Omri didn't answer. Every time he thought of the Indian battle, it took away from his overwhelming pleasure in the one with the skinheads.

"Where's Boone?" he asked suddenly.

"I sent him back too. He asked me to. Said the odd gunfight and saloon brawl would be a rest cure after all he's been through . . . He said he'd like to see us soon, when things have quieted down."

"What about his horse?"

"Oh, yes. I gave him the one that English cavalry officer was riding." Patrick chuckled. "You should have heard him swear when I flicked him off! Boone was really pleased. Said he's a beaut. Really, he was happy with it. And I bet the horse'll be happier with him than with that snooty redcoat."

When they reached the room, all was quiet. The candle had burnt out, so Little Bear had had to stop his dancing and chanting for the dead. One fire was out, the other was burning low. The Indians, including the wounded, were all asleep, except Little Bear, who sat cross-legged by the fire. Bright Stars was asleep beside him, the baby in the crook of her arm.

Patrick struck a match and Little Bear looked up.

"We've brought food," Omri said.

"No eat," said the Indian.

Omri didn't press him. He just poured a toothpaste

capful of hot chocolate and put it beside him with a piece of potato.

The match went out. They sat together in the dark, with just the embers of the fire. The boys drank their chocolate. For a long time nobody spoke.

Then Little Bear said: "Why Omri bring Little Bear?"

For the first time in two days, Omri thought of his prize. It had gone completely from his mind. Now it seemed so trivial, he was ashamed to mention it.

"Something good happened to me, which was partly to do with you, and I wanted to tell you about it."

"What good thing happen?"

"I wrote a story about you and Boone and it—well, it was good."

"Omri write truth of Little Bear?"

"Yes, it was all true."

"Omri write Little Bear kill own people?"

"Of course not!"

"You write before this happen. Next time, write Little Bear kill own braves."

"You didn't. The now-guns killed them. You couldn't know."

"Then, Little Bear fool!" came his bitter voice out of the dark.

There was a silence. Then Patrick said, "We were the fools, not you."

"Yes," said Omri. "We should have known better. We shouldn't have interfered."

"Inta-fear? Omri not afraid."

"We should have let you alone."

"Let alone, Little Bear die from French gun."

There was a pause. Then Omri said, "You did beat the Algonquins."

"Yes. Beat Algonquin thief. Not beat French."

"Yeah, that was a pity," said Patrick feelingly, "after all that."

"Fewer dead the better," muttered Omri.

"Good kill French!" Little Bear exclaimed, sounding more like his old self. "Kill French next time."

"But not with the now-guns."

After a silence, Little Bear said, "Now-guns good. Shoot far. Now Little Bear know shoot far. Next time not put own braves where bullet go. Omri give now-guns, take back!"

The embers of the fire flared a little. Bright Stars had risen to throw on another curl of wax. Now she crouched beside Little Bear and looked into his face.

"No," she said clearly.

He looked at her.

"What no?"

She spoke to him softly and earnestly in their own language. He scowled in the firelight.

"What does she say, Little Bear?"

"Wife say, not use now-guns. Soon braves forget skill with bow. Woman not want son grow up without Indian skill. She say now-gun kill too many, too easy. No honor for chief or chief's son."

"What do you think?"

"Omri give now-guns if Little Bear think good?"

Omri shook his head.

"Then, what for I fight with wife? Give wife own way. Peace in longhouse, till next enemy come. Then maybe wife sorry!"

He scowled at her. She smiled, bent down and picked up the baby and laid it in his arms. He sat looking down at it.

"What's his name?" Omri asked.

"Name must mean much," mused Little Bear. "What 'Omri' mean?"

"Omri was a king. In the old days."

"Omri name for big chief?"

Omri nodded.

"Then, Little Bear son name too for chief. For father, Little Bear, had first horse in all tribe. Call him Tall Bear. He sit high on horse, more high than all brave."

Suddenly he clutched the baby to his chest, and turned his face upward with closed eyes as if bearing a strong pain.

"When son grow, Little Bear tell that Omri write story! Little Bear live in story even when gone to ancestors. *That* give honor, make son proud of father!"

"He'll be proud of you, Little Bear. Without any help from me."

Little Bear looked up at him. Then he stood up. The fire put out a sudden flare. He stood there, feet apart, his body glowing, his stern face for once untroubled.

"Omri good," he said loudly. "Give *orenda* back to Little Bear!"

Orenda. The life force.

And he held his son up high in both hands, as if offering him to the future.

ABOUT THE AUTHOR

Lynne Reid Banks was born in London in 1929 and spent World War II on the Canadian prairies as a "war guest." On returning home, she studied drama and acted for five years. She then went into journalism, becoming the first woman TV news reporter in Britain in 1955. In 1960 her first novel, *The L-Shaped Room*, was published, and it was later filmed. In 1962 she emigrated to Israel, where she married, had three sons, and spent eight years living on a kibbutz and teaching English. She returned to London with her family in 1971 and became a full-time writer. She has written more than forty books, mainly novels for adults and young readers, including the award-winning Indian in the Cupboard series; *I, Houdini; The Farthest-Away Mountain;* and *The Fairy Rebel*. Lynne Reid Banks lives in a three-hundred-year-old farmhouse in Dorset, England, with her husband. She often travels and visits schools at home and abroad.

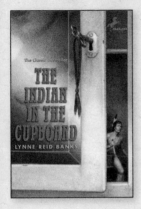

THE INDIAN IN THE CUPBOARD

THE RETURN OF THE INDIAN

THE SECRET OF THE INDIAN

LYNNE REID BANKS

GRADES 4–7

themes

Friendship • Trust/Secrets • Loneliness
Lying • Bullying • Stereotypes

curriculum connections

Language Arts • Social Studies/Native American Interest
Math • Science • Art

PB: 978-0-375-85523-8

PB: 978-0-375-84753-0

PB: 978-0-375-85524-5

about the books

Omri receives two unusual birthday gifts in *The Indian in the Cupboard*. One is a plastic Indian and the other a metal cupboard with a key on a red ribbon. When Omri puts the Indian in the cupboard and turns the key, the Indian comes to life and Omri's life changes forever. The secret becomes a burden so Omri sends the Indian home, and vows to abstain from using the magic key. A year has passed and in *The Return of the Indian,* the desire to see his Indian is so strong that Omri takes the key and brings him back to life. This time, his Indian needs help that is almost beyond the magic that Omri creates. *The Secret of the Cupboard* brings another adventure. Omri discovers that he can time travel with the help of the magic key. His friend Patrick wants to visit the Western town of his plastic cowboy, Boone. Omri agrees to send him back in time, but when Patrick returns he brings back more than an adventure.

pre-reading activity

Divide students into small discussion groups. Ask them to jot down how they think Native Americans lived in the 1800s. What is the basis of their knowledge? Then send the group to the library media center and ask them to verify their facts. Ask each group to make a true or false test for the class about Native American life.

vocabulary/
use of language

The Indian in the Cupboard

defiant (p. 8), *coherent* (p. 8), *bandolier* (p.13), *ravenously* (p. 24), *commando* (p. 36), *pommel* (p. 43), *mulish* (p. 94), *prostrate* (p.116), *infinitesimal* (p.166), and *stupefaction* (p. 167)

The Return of the Indian

gauntlet (p. 2), *antagonism* (p. 2), *magnanimous* (p. 15), *stalwart* (p. 15), *extricated* (p. 27), *proprietor* (p. 52), *antiquated* (p. 60), *enigmatic* (p. 61), *hygienic* (p. 62), *derelict* (p. 70), *pinioned* (p. 73), *lethal* (p. 89), *imperious* (p.101), *decorously* (p. 96), *delirious* (p.111), *harangue* (p. 119), *interlude* (p. 121), *scrimmage* (p. 126), and *carnage* (p.160)

The Secret of the Indian

interrogation (p. 5), *pockmarked* (p. 7), *peremptorily* (p.10), *expostulated* (p.11), *salubrious* (p.12), *formidable* (p. 30), *akimbo* (p. 47), *fatalism* (p. 48), *stalwart* (p. 54), *supine* (p. 54), *oblivion* (p. 61), *phlegmatic* (p. 66), *consigning* (p.78), *incredulous* (p. 83), *stupendous* (p.142), *devastated* (p.154), *evasive* (p.162), and *discomfiture* (p.163)

thematic connections
questions for group discussions

Friendship—Describe Omri and Patrick's friendship. There are many times when their friendship is tested. At what point do they face the greatest test? How does their friendship change when Patrick moves away? In *The Return of the Indian,* Patrick acts as if he doesn't remember anything about the magic cupboard. Discuss whether Patrick has simply outgrown Omri and the magic cupboard.

Trust/Secrets—Discuss the relationship between trust and secrets. Explain Omri's strong urge to tell his secret. Omri thought that he could trust Patrick, so he told him about the magic cupboard. There are times in all three novels that Patrick breaks that trust. What is the ultimate breach of trust in *The Indian in the Cupboard*? Omri agrees to take Little Bear to school and keep him in his pocket all day. What are the consequences that Omri faces if his secret is revealed? At what point in *The Secret of the Indian* does Omri begin trusting Emma with the secret of the Indian?

Loneliness—Explain Omri's statement in *The Return of the Indian* that secrets cause loneliness. How do Omri and Patrick handle Little Bear's loneliness? Describe Boone's loneliness. Patrick finally admits that he keeps Boone in his pocket at all times. Discuss whether this has anything to do with loneliness and the life that Patrick left behind when he and his mother moved to another town.

Lying—Explain how the lies that Omri tells are related to the secret that he is keeping. How do the lies turn Omri and Patrick into heroes in *The Secret of the Indian*?

Bullying—Omri's parents move to a different neighborhood in *The Return of the Indian,* a neighborhood filled with bullies. How does Little Bear give Omri courage to face the bullies? Who would Little Bear say are his bullies? What about Boone? Who are his bullies? How do Little Bear and Boone handle their bullies?

Stereotypes—Ask students to discuss the meaning of stereotyping. In *The Indian in the Cupboard,* Omri says, "This Indian—his Indian—was behaving in every way like a real live Indian brave." (p. 12) How does Omri expect a "real live Indian brave" to behave? Why is stereotyping wrong? How does Little Bear change Omri's opinion of Indians?

connecting to the curriculum

Language Arts—Omri wins a prize for his short story called "The Plastic Indian." Have students write the story that Omri might have written.

Boone speaks in a Western dialect. Read the first paragraph on page 81 in *The Return of the Indian,* and write Boone's words in standard English. Then discuss how the dialect contributes to the authenticity of the book.

Illustration © 2010 by Tristan Elwell

Social Studies—Little Bear is involved in the French and Indian War. Have students use reference books or Internet resources to find out about this war. What caused the war? Who were the enemy? Who won the war? Then write a brief narrative about the war from Little Bear's perspective.

Little Bear is of the Iroquois tribe. He wants Omri to understand the difference in his tribe and the Algonquin tribe. Ask students to research both tribes and make a chart that records their differences.

Math—Omri wins a cash prize for his story "The Plastic Indian." As a class, convert the £300.00 that Omri wins to U.S. dollars. Then plan a budget for Omri. What will he purchase? How much will he save?

Science—Little Bear and Boone are wounded and Omri realizes that they need a doctor. Have the class research medical treatments for battle wounds in the 1800s. What types of anesthesia did they use for surgery? What herbs and plants did the Native Americans use as medicines? Have students write a brief article called "How Native Americans Practiced Medicine in the 1800s."

Art—Ask students to construct a miniature longhouse for Little Bear. Have them research the symbols of the Iroquois tribe and paint those symbols on Little Bear's new house.

booktalks
Hook young readers!

The Indian in the Cupboard

Omri receives two gifts for his birthday that he simply has no use for. One is a secondhand plastic Indian and the other is a white metal cupboard that had been discarded as rubbish. Then quite by accident Omri discovers that the key to the cupboard is magic. What happens inside the cupboard is so unbelievable that Omri knows that it has to be his secret.

The Return of the Indian

Omri realizes that Little Bear, his Indian, is in danger so he sends him home and gives the magic key to his mother to wear around her neck. A year has passed and the urge to see Little Bear is so strong that Omri takes the key and brings his plastic Indian back to life. When he sees Little Bear, Omri is forced to make the toughest decision of his life. How did his game become such a nightmare?

The Secret of the Indian

It's one thing for Omri to bring plastic toys to life, but it's quite another thing to discover that his magic key can transport himself and his friend Patrick to another time. What is life like in the frontier age of their plastic friends? Patrick finds out when he time travels back and spends a little time with his cowboy friend, Boone. But what Patrick brings home is more than a great adventure.

internet resources

FACTS FOR KIDS

Haudenosaunee (Iroquois) Indians
www.bigorrin.org/iroquois_kids.htm

This site offers a fact sheet about the Iroquois tribe.

Algonquin Indians
www.bigorrin.org/algonquin_kids.htm

This site offers a fact sheet about the Algonquin Tribe.

THE WILD WEST

www.thewildwest.org/interface/index.php?action=186

This site provides information about the Wild West, cowboys, and legends.

Guide prepared by Pat Scales, Children's Literature Consultant, Greenville, South Carolina.

related titles

BY THEME

GARY PAULSEN

The Time Hackers
Yearling PB:
978-0-553-48788-6

Grades 5 up
Adventure • Time Travel

GLORIA WHELAN

Next Spring an Oriole
Random House PB:
978-0-394-89125-5

Night of the Full Moon
Random House PB:
978-0-679-87276-4

The Shadow of the Wolf
Random House PB:
978-0-679-88108-7

Grades 2–5
Adventure • Native Americans

ELIZABETH WINTHROP

The Castle in the Attic ⌒
Yearling PB:
978-0-440-40941-0

The Battle for the Castle ⌒
Yearling PB:
978-0-440-40942-7

Grades 5–8
Adventure • Time Travel • Trust

⌒ = Listening Library audio available

more books
BY LYNNE REID BANKS

The Fairy Rebel

Yearling PB:
978-0-440-41925-9

Grades 4–7
Fantasy • Fairy Tales & Fables
Family & Relationships • Good vs. Evil

I, Houdini

Yearling PB:
978-0-440-41924-2

Grades 4–7
Adventure • Animals • Humor

Tiger, Tiger

Laurel-Leaf PB:
978-0-440-42044-6

Grades 7–11
Historical Fiction
Acceptance & Belonging
Animals

a conversation with
lynne reid banks

Q: It is written that you were a reluctant reader when you were young. At what point did you become a reader? Is there a person that led you toward books?

A: It would be truer to say that I was a lazy reader. I liked to be read to. But I always loved stories. My mother turned me on to them and she must have induced me to begin reading for myself. I can't remember learning to read, or ever not being able to.

Q: When did you realize that writing was your calling? Did you like writing stories when you were young?

A: I was inventing stories before I could write them—I would dictate them to my mother. After I learned to write, I simply was always writing something—diaries, letters, stories, articles, plays, books, and much more besides. My earliest ambition was to be an actress, but even while I was doing that, I was always writing.

Q: What book do you remember most from your childhood?

A: What one book? I suppose, Kipling's *The Jungle Book,* but there were many others, mainly about ponies, dogs, and bears!

Q: You must have had a vivid imagination as a child. What was your favorite game of pretend?

A: I imagined that I was a little girl in India who had to keep house for myself and eat exotic things. I always imagined living in a hut in the jungle and eating off leaves.

Q: What book is on your bedside table?

A: At this moment it happens to be *Acting Up* by David Hare, with *The Victorians* by Vita Sackville-West underneath it and under that is my autobiography in a folder. It's called "An L-Shaped Life."

Q: **How do you answer critics who take issue with the way you portray Indians in your books? In _The Secret of the Indian,_ Omri does say to Mr. Johnson when he says "Red Indian" that he should say American Indian or Native American. Did you add this to the story to answer the critics?**

A: Not exactly. I wrote the books about seven years apart, and they were the years (the eighties) when Indians themselves asked to be called Native Americans. This development either hadn't happened or I hadn't heard about it in 1980 when I wrote the first book. As to what the critics of my books have had to say, I'm afraid I think it's silly and misjudged. Little Bear is a role model any race would be proud of: brave, independent, sober, devoted to his culture and his people. Among other virtues.

Q: **How much research did you do about Native American tribes before writing these books?**

A: Not much for the first one, but as the series went on, I became more aware of the pitfalls and more determined not to hurt anyone. For _Key to the Indian_ (the final volume), I traveled to Canada to stay in an Iroquois village, and read everything I could lay hands on about the Five Nations.

Q: **Did you always know that you wanted to write sequels to _The Indian in the Cupboard_?**

A: No. I never planned it as a series, which is why it took over 15 years. I planned a sixth book when Omri would be grown up, but the battles I had to fight to defend the earlier books put me off.

Teachers @ RANDOM

www.randomhouse.com/teachers

The ultimate online resource for educators to
help bring quality literature into the classroom

Reading Programs

Mini sites featuring classroom
connections and activities for
programs, including Step into
Reading, Stepping Stones, Yearling,
and Dragonfly.

BOOKNOTES
Educator Guides

Over 350 exclusive guides with
innovative thematic and
curriculum connections written
by leaders in the field.

Search Capabilities

Find the books you are
looking for by searching over
140 themes and holidays by
format or grade level.

Author and Illustrator Biographies

Over 150 extensive
biographies, exclusive
interviews, and fun facts
ideal for author studies.

Classroom CAST ▶

Video Podcasting Program

MAGIC TREE HOUSE
Mary Pope Osborne

The Edge CHRONICLES Paul Stewart
Chris Riddell

THE FIVE ANCESTORS
Jeff Stone

MAUDE MARCH
Audrey Couloumbis

BABYMOUSE
Jennifer L. Holm
Matthew Holm

Random House Children's Books is delighted to share ClassroomCast— a marketing initiative that provides entertaining and curriculum-based videos for a classroom environment in support of leading Random House authors and series. ClassroomCast will serve as an essential resource for teachers who are looking for ways to bring multimedia into their lessons and bring literature to life! These videos show the authors discussing their work, research, and how they go about writing their books.

And best of all—it's free! Log on to **www.rhcbclassroomcast.com** for details! Look for additional downloadable resources for the classroom to support key lesson plans and get kids reading!

The ClassroomCast program already includes Mary Pope Osborne, Paul Stewart and Chris Riddell, Jeff Stone, Audrey Couloumbis, and Jennifer and Matthew Holm.

YEARLING

For over 40 years, Yearling has been the leading name in classic and award-winning literature for young readers. Educators count on Yearling paperbacks for dynamic and engaging stories that will inspire students and generate rich discussion in the classroom. With over 25 Newbery Award and Newbery Honor winning titles, favorite authors and characters, and a wide variety of genres, there are books for every unique reader that will lead to a lifetime love of reading.

Visit **www.randomhouse.com/teachers** for
free educator guides to these books.